# SWEET BREEZE RESORT

## GETAWAY BAY RESORT ROMANCE, BOOK 6

### ELANA JOHNSON

ISBN-13: 978-1-63876-015-3

# ONE

GINA JACKSON WHISTLED while she worked in the corner of the suite, her measuring tape making a metallic crinkling sound as she tried to get it all the way against the wall.

She and Owen Church, the general manager here at Sweet Breeze, had talked about taking these boring, blah closets into something spectacular for the longer-stay guests at the premier hotel and resort in Getaway Bay.

Gina Jackson could still taste the dill cream cheese she'd eaten on her bagel over an hour ago. She really needed a mint—and for her blasted tape measure to stop acting all wonky.

The metallic crinkling sound grated against her nerves as she shook the end of it into the corner. The closets at Sweet Breeze Resort and Hotel were nothing like any she'd worked on before. They were almost like rooms of their own, and while Gina had taken closet organization into a billion-dollar business, her nerves squirmed at the thought of messing up this job.

Thus, her bagel breakfast with the boss over this project at Sweet Breeze, Owen Church. *Boss* ran through her mind. She and Owen were definitely working together, though he wasn't really her boss. He was the general manager at the hotel, and his opinion was all that mattered. Gina had noticed that the owner of the hotel—Fisher DuPont—didn't call nearly as many shots as Owen did.

She'd marveled at that for a while, as she finished a couple of other jobs on the island and contemplated not returning to the mainland at all.

She'd seen Owen and Fisher together, felt their energy, and envied the complete trust between them. She used to have a partner like that, but the lure of money and power had been too great, and the betrayal coursing through Gina definitely still stung.

The tape measure simply wouldn't cooperate today, and she wasn't sure the ideas she'd discussed with Owen while he smeared strawberry cream cheese over a cinnamon raisin bagel would even work.

She'd never understand his weird food combinations, and they'd been sharing a lot of meals together lately. Most in his office, or here at the hotel after their morning run.

Gina couldn't seem to get Owen out of her mind, not even long enough to measure a simple space, something she could normally do with just the naked eye.

She sighed, determined not to let the handsome man distract her from the job, and not to let the job—a huge, multi-million dollar job that could establish her in the hotel industry— consume her very existence.

With her foot, she stomped the end of the measuring device into the carpet and finally pulled the tape taut. "Seventeen feet, two inches," she muttered to herself. And that was just the depth of this closet. The width had to be easily twice that.

Fisher had designed the hotel to be the best of its kind, but he hadn't truly thought of those who might want a long-term stay. As more and more businessmen and women came to Getaway Bay, he'd realized a need for such a suite.

Well, Gina suspected it was Owen who'd noticed the need, run it all by Fisher, and then started remodeling their nicer suites into long-term stay apartments.

Gina had been contracted to take some of the existing space and make it into a closet. With the smell of fresh paint from the new kitchen area just around the corner, she once again pushed against the anxiety that she couldn't do this job. That it was too big for her. That her normal master bedroom closet in a single-family home in Dallas simply hadn't provided her the experience she needed for a job of this magnitude, on this scale.

Sure, she'd done the five rooms at the bed and breakfast down the beach. The owner had been thrilled, but they were basically bedrooms with normal sized closets Gina had simply taken up a notch.

But Fisher's wife had been so complimentary that this job at Sweet Breeze had basically fallen into Gina's lap. She couldn't say no, even if she felt leagues out of her, well, league.

She took a few more measurements and consulted her catalog for systems that might fit. It would be ultra-expensive to have a custom-built organization system, but she couldn't find anything that seemed like it would work. Everything in her catalog was too small for a space like this.

Sighing, she left the bedroom and went into the main living area, which was in a state of construction. "Maybe the closet doesn't need to be that big," she said to the drop cloth protecting the tile floor in the kitchen area. The appliances still had plastic on them, and she had to be out of the room in an hour so the painters could finish.

Then it was just loading the room with the furniture, the new linens, drapes, accessories—oh, and her closeting system.

Desperation pushed against her tongue, but she swallowed it back. She would not panic. She could do it.

"You can do this," she said aloud and went back into the bedroom. This suite sat in the corner on the fifth floor. Owen wanted two dozen long-term stay apartments, some one-bedroom suites like the one where Gina stood now, and some with two bedrooms. She'd been through those, but she hadn't been able to take measurements or spend much time in the room, as it had been in the middle of the demolition process to turn the suite into an apartment.

"Maybe the closet is just too big," she said to the stark room, something Owen had said that morning. They'd gone over a few designs, and he'd liked them all. She'd expressed her concerns over the size, the measurements, and making sure it looked high-end like he wanted, but remained functional—her trademark.

*Everyone should have a closet that works for them.* That was her company motto, one she'd written herself for Classy Closets, and that she stuck to on every job she took.

After all, it made no sense to hire a professional organizer and licensed interior designer to get something that wasn't even usable.

She stepped around the scaffolding in the room the painters used and shook out her measuring tape again. "There could be a separate dressing area here," she said, thinking out loud. "It would shave off a few feet, and give me access to the twelve-foot systems."

Gina turned in a slow circle, imagining the shelving, the hanging racks, the spot the iron would go—with a fold-out board that disappeared seamlessly into the wall. She saw the island in the middle, an easy spot for travelers to put their bags and unpack for their stay. Extra towels, robes, and linens could go in the cupboards on the island so guests wouldn't have to call and wait—or bother housekeeping—for basic needs.

She envisioned a shoe rack down the wall, as well as a high hanging rack for suits and formal dresses. Then, through the door, the dressing area, with full-length mirrors on two walls.

"That's it," she said. "That's what we need in here." Excitement coursed through her that she'd solved this problem. Now, she just needed to talk to Owen, because this wasn't an easy fix for him. She was proposing more construction, more expenses with another door, mirrors, and that extra rack.

Still, she could see the closet in her mind, and it was

exactly what this suite needed. She wasn't the best sales-person on the planet, but she'd draw the blueprint for him and see what he said.

Owen loved blueprints, and Gina grinned to herself as she twisted to go find him. She'd gotten turned around in the room as the closet came to life inside her mind, and she stubbed her toe against the scaffolding.

"How's it going?"

Gina yelped, first in pain, and then fright at the deep male voice. She hopped on her good foot, but that didn't help her keep her balance.

She knew she was going down—and right in front of those dark, deep, dreamy eyes of Owen's—before she did. She frantically reached for the scaffolding—anything to anchor herself—though her brain screamed at her that it was a bad idea. The last thing she needed was to pull the metal structure down on top of her.

She missed anyway, blast her poor coordination. The beau-tiful closet disappeared from her mind as she flopped back-ward, Owen's voice somewhere beyond her going, "Gina."

Everything happened so fast, and while Gina didn't consider herself old by any means, her thirty-six-year-old body protested at the hardness of the floor against her tail-bone, shoulders, and head.

Owen appeared in her vision. "Are you okay? I didn't mean to startle you." He wore a look of pure panic, sorrow, and compassion.

All Gina could do was stare into those eyes that followed her into her dreams and shake her head.

"You're not okay?" His gaze sharpened and he pulled out his phone. One tap. Two swipes, and he said, "Jillian, it's Owen. I need medical on the fifth floor, suite 512."

Gina kept shaking her head. "I'm okay."

Owen looked very doubtful and kept his phone at his ear. "Gina Jackson fell." He reached out with his free hand and swept his fingers across her face, letting them linger in her hair.

She couldn't read his expression at all, but he jolted away from her as if he'd been shocked and sat back on his heels. "She's talking...five minutes. Thank you, Jillian."

He hung up and hovered over her again. "Someone is coming, Gina. Five minutes."

As if she hadn't heard him already. "I'm fine," she said again, this time pushing herself into a seated position. At least all her running and beach yoga had made it possible for her to do such a thing. She'd taken up exercise after Ian, the partner who'd betrayed her, had left Classy Closets, taking so much of Gina and her company with him that she hardly recognized herself anymore.

He certainly wouldn't recognize her now, not fifty pounds lighter, with the dark hair she got from a bottle, and more success than she'd achieved previously, simply by doing everything herself. No partners.

Owen touched her face again, drawing Gina back to this embarrassing moment. "Did you hit your head?"

Gina reached up and touched the back of her head, where a lump was forming. "Yeah. Right here."

Owen's fingers probed through her hair gently, sending

sparks down her spine and fire through her blood. "Ah, yes. It's not too big though."

Maybe if she said her back hurt, he'd rub it. Gina gazed at him, wondering at the powerful current between them. She'd always found him handsome. Kind. Dedicated. Loyal. And he was probably the only person on the planet who worked more than she did.

"I just came to see how things were going," he said, letting his fingers linger in her hair.

She leaned into his touch, her eyes drifting halfway closed. Could he feel this energy between them? What if she was the only one who felt like she was falling toward an unknown source of gravity, with no way to catch herself? "I had an idea."

"I have one too." His voice rumbled through Gina, and she barely had time to open her eyes before his lips touched hers.

A gasp pulled through her whole body, and suddenly nothing hurt anymore.

# TWO

OWEN PRESSED his lips to Gina's, enjoying the warmth of them, the way they fit against his. One second later, he realized what he'd done.

*Idiot.*

He pulled back as panic raced through him. Gina still sat there on the floor, and when her eyes opened, they were filled with confusion.

"I'm sorry," he said, standing and walking backward. "I...I don't know what that was." Oh, he knew what it was. His base instincts had taken over, when he'd been pushing them back for weeks and weeks. Months, even. But running with her in the morning simply wasn't enough anymore. Inventing meetings where she had to come sit across from him in his office wasn't either.

He liked Gina Jackson, and it wasn't on friendly terms. Or maybe too friendly of terms. Owen was pretty confused himself.

"I'll go see if medical is here yet." Owen got the heck out of that bedroom, foolishness racing through him with the speed of a stock car.

"What was that?" he muttered to himself. And had she liked it?

"That wasn't even long enough to like," he said as he pulled open the door and checked the hallway for medical. He really needed someone in the room with him, or he might kiss her again. Really kiss her, hold on this time, stroke his lips against hers.

He banished the thought, replacing it with the image of his two sons. *Two sons.* Two *teenage* sons, one of whom was set to graduate from high school in only a few months.

He let the door close behind him and he rested his back against it. Gina couldn't possibly like him, not the way he wanted her to. She wasn't even a permanent fixture on the island.

*Yet,* his mind whispered, apparently undeterred in its mission to convince him he might have a chance with the beautiful brunette.

But he knew he didn't have a chance, and not simply because of his kids. Gina had a way of putting up walls between them, and Owen wasn't even sure she knew she was doing it. But she'd just been hurt, and all her defenses had gone down. He'd acted irrationally, and he closed his eyes and prayed quickly that she wouldn't say anything to Fisher.

Owen wouldn't lose his job or anything, but Fisher had been pushing him to date for over a year now. Once he'd married Stacey, suddenly everyone needed to find wedded bliss.

Well, Owen had been there once, thank you very much. And that had ended badly, with another man with his wife, in their bed. No, Owen didn't need to repeat any of that, and though it had been almost a decade, sometimes his heart still cringed at what his wife had done.

Because she hadn't just abandoned him for a man with untold riches and yachts and a life of luxury. She'd freely given Owen fully custody of their sons, barely sending birthday cards on time. In fact, she'd missed Cooper's last birthday by a week. Owen had been doing as much damage control as possible since the day she left.

And he still wasn't sure why he and the boys hadn't been enough for her. It wasn't like they didn't have money. Owen came from the real estate business, and he had millions in the bank too.

Not billions like Fisher, or Marshall, or even Gina, all members of the Nine-0 Club Fisher hosted at the hotel some-times. But definitely enough for his wife to take vacations and lie by the pool while he worked.

Ultimately, he'd concluded the flaw was within him, and instead of facing what it might be, he'd buried himself in work.

"Owen?"

He opened his eyes to two men walking toward him, both carrying large duffle bags.

"In here," he said, opening the door. "She's in the bedroom, to the right." He let the medical team in first, following them to find Gina sitting on a folding chair just inside the door.

"You shouldn't have moved," he said, barely looking at her. Embarrassment heated his face, and he could not believe he'd kissed her and then abandoned her in a construction zone. For a forty-six-year-old, he should know better.

"I told you, I'm fine." Her bright blue eyes shot lasers at him, but he absorbed the power of them, wondering what color her hair would be if she didn't get it dyed every month.

He let the medical team talk to her, check her pupils, and give her some pain medication. When they prepared to leave, Owen pretended to get a very important text and ducked out before them.

He'd barely made it to the elevator when he received a real message. From Gina: *I need to talk to you. When's a good time?*

*Now*, he wanted to type out. Instead, he thumbed *Never* as the elevator door opened. But he couldn't send that either. He worked with her. He'd have to see her again. They had twenty-four rooms to work on. Thirty closets. Months and months to go until this renovation was complete.

Plus, they were supposed to run together the next morning.

Owen had never particularly enjoyed running, but when the gorgeous woman who'd been the first to make his heart pump faster than normal asked, he'd gone straight to the shoe store and bought a pair of sneakers that should get him through a couple of marathons.

They'd been running together for months now, and

Owen still hadn't found a way to ask Gina to dinner where work wasn't involved.

"Kissing her probably told her a lot." He cringed as he got off the elevator and hurried past the check-in counter, Jason who was on security today, and down the hall to his office.

Only then did he delete the *never* on his phone and type out a much more political and aloof *whenever works for you. I'm in my office.*

————

The day passed, like days do, and Gina didn't show up to talk to him. Fisher did, several times, and Owen signed things, made phone calls, and filled out his calendar with Cooper's basketball games. He hadn't missed a single one since his son had made the team last year, and he didn't plan to this season either. Besides his job, his sons were all he had, and he'd devoted everything he had to Sweet Breeze, Zach, and Cooper.

Sure, he worked more than he probably needed to. But he liked the way it filled the hours, liked that his sons came and hung out at the pools with their friends, liked that they could grab food from one of the restaurants and eat it in his office.

His radio beeped and someone said, "Owen, there's a disturbance by the museum."

He stood, knowing he couldn't make it through one day without something happening. "On my way. Jason?"

"Meet you at the elevator."

Jason held the door until Owen stepped on, and he nodded at the man. He and Lexie, a long-time Nine-0 Club member had just gotten married, and he'd proved to be an excellent employee.

"What does disturbance mean?" Jason asked as the elevator whisked them up a few floors.

"Probably someone who's had too much to drink." That was the cause of almost all the problems at Sweet Breeze. Owen had given up alcohol a couple of months after Linda had left. It had dulled his nerves and mind until the divorce was final, but then he realized his sons needed him. Only eight and five at the time, they deserved a father. So when he'd come out of his bedroom, drunk, to find Zach had made grilled cheese sandwiches for him and Cooper—and burnt them and filled the house with smoke—Owen had given up drinking completely. And without women, he lived a perfectly pure and chaste life—and was pretty happy doing so.

But it wasn't someone who'd drunk too much causing a problem outside the museum. It was Gina Jackson.

"Gina?" He approached slowly, pausing altogether and holding up his hand for Jason to stop too when she spun toward them.

Her eyes were wild, and she held up a fistful of papers. "This says I can get in the museum for free."

Owen remained passive, calm. This wasn't the Gina he knew. She'd definitely hit her head harder than anyone had thought. When she saw him, she quieted, her hand lowering to her side. "Owen?"

"Those coupons expired six months ago, sir," the

museum attendant said. "I tried explaining it to her." He looked at Gina with wariness. "She didn't seem to believe me."

"It's okay, Santiago. I'll take her to my office." He extended his hand to her, almost like he would a child. "Come on, Gina."

She came toward him, lacing her fingers through his while Jason watched. Owen wished every muscle in his body wouldn't sigh, but they did. Then his nerves danced with joy that he was *holding hands with Gina Jackson.*

*She's not well,* he thought, but the rest of his body— including his heart, which continued to beat out a rhythm that was entirely too excited—didn't seem to care.

"Call Doctor Blithe," he whispered to Jason once they'd returned to the first floor. "She hit her head earlier, and I'm afraid she might have a concussion."

Jason nodded slightly, and Owen continued with Gina down the hall to his office. Once they were sealed inside, Owen busied himself with ordering her favorite fried cheese from the bistro on the third floor, sending a text to Zach that he had an issue to deal with and would be home later, and then asking Gina for the coupons.

"I didn't think you liked the museum," he said. He'd mentioned it to her once, and she'd shot him down pretty fast, citing museums as "boring."

She watched him with those blue eyes, and Owen chose not to look away. Seconds passed, and he had to believe she felt something between them too. It was simply too strong *not* to feel it.

"I'm sorry I kissed you," he said, thinking she probably

needed an explanation. "I...something came over me in the moment, and it was wrong."

Gina reached up and brushed her fingertips against her lips, almost like she could remember the barely-there touch of his mouth. "Like something came over me at the museum." She blinked, confusion rushing through her eyes. "My head hurts."

"I know." He smiled at her, what he hoped was a genuine, caring, kind smile. "Doctor Blithe is on her way." He opened the top drawer in his desk and took out a bottle of painkillers. "And you should take a few of these." He slid the bottle toward her and reached under his desk to the mini fridge he kept filled with water bottles.

Tears filled Gina's eyes as she took the ice cold bottle of water and tapped some pills into her palm. "Owen, you always know what to do and when to do it."

"Oh, that's not true." Or he wouldn't have kissed her like that earlier.

"I was going to tell you this morning," she said, pausing with the ibuprofen still in her hand. "We need to redesign the closets. They're simply too big." Some of the papers in her hands got smoothed onto his desktop. "I've redrawn the blueprints for you."

Owen loved Gina's handwriting, the clever way she had with space and design, and how she could make something as simple as a closet come to life in black and white. He smiled fondly at the pages covered in black ink and pulled them toward him. "Let's see what you've come up with this time."

# THREE

GINA'S HEAD pounded like someone was banging on it with a plastic mallet. The way she used to abuse the xylophones in her high school band. She closed her eyes, but that only made a terrible sense of vertigo overtake her.

Owen glanced at her and back at the blueprints. Gina couldn't get a read on him, and she thought about that microsecond where he'd kissed her earlier that morning.

At least she didn't have to wonder if he liked her. A tiny smile touched those same lips Owen's had, and that caused her head to hurt too.

"I don't think I can drive myself home," she finally said. "How soon are you heading out? Could you give me a ride?"

"Doctor Blithe is coming," he said, shifting one paper under the other. She'd drawn the closeting system for the single bedroom apartments a bit different than for the two bedroom units.

She didn't dare tell him she'd gone into the construction zones on the seventh and eighth floor. He would not be happy about that, even if she was healthy. And they both knew she wasn't.

"You're not even arguing," Owen said.

Gina shrugged, wondering if she could share some of her past with him. "I don't like doctors," she said. And she didn't, but it probably wasn't for the same reasons as other people.

Owen didn't return his attention to the blueprints, but kept his eyes on her. "Oh? Why not?"

Gina swallowed, her mouth dry and chalky. She couldn't remember the last thing she ate, or when she'd last had a drink. She lifted the water bottle to her lips and swallowed the pills. Still Owen hadn't looked away.

"I had a bad experience as a teenager." She gazed right back at him, wanting to open the door all the way, beckon him inside, share everything with him.

At the same time, she knew what would happen if she did. And she rather liked this island and was considering staying.

"I grew up in the foster system," she blurted. She almost covered her mouth with her hand like she'd just said something awful and embarrassing.

Surprise mixed with compassion in Owen's expression. "I'm sorry," he said. "Where?"

"My home state, Texas."

"You're from Dallas, right?"

Her company was in Dallas, but it was easier to say, "Yes," than try to tell him about the tiny town where she bounced from house to house in the middle of Texas Hill Country.

"No good experiences with any of your families?"

Gina didn't want to talk about her time in the foster system. Thankfully, someone knocked on the door and Owen practically leapt across the desk to answer it.

"Thank you, Ben." He took the tray, and Gina really hoped it was the fried cheese from that bistro she liked. She couldn't even think of when he'd ordered that.

"I'll put your tip on your paycheck." Owen smiled at the waiter and closed the door. He presented her with the food, and drew off the top of the cloche to reveal the item she wanted most.

Gina smiled and shook her head. "You really are amazing."

Owen didn't respond as he moved behind her and retook his place at the desk. "I assume you haven't eaten in a while." He flicked a glance toward her and studied his phone. "Probably not since our bagels this morning."

She liked his use of "our," but she didn't want to confirm that he'd spoken true. Then she'd have to say she'd been in the forbidden two-bedroom units, taking measurements and dodging two-by-fours while her head felt like it was cleaving in two.

Another knock and Owen let in the doctor while Gina finished off her first cheese stick.

"Hello, Joyce." Owen kissed the doctor on the cheek. "Gina here hit her head this morning."

Gina wanted to say she was fine, but deep down, she knew she wasn't.

"Did you call someone?" Joyce Blithe had to be close to sixty-five-years-old, but she looked like a no-nonsense kind of woman. She set her medical bag on Owen's desk next to the plate of fried cheese and pulled out a stethoscope.

Why doctors always started by listening to the heart, Gina didn't know. She hadn't hurt her heart. But she let Doctor Blithe listen, ask her questions, and look in her eyes, her ears, her throat, all of it.

"It's a mild concussion," she said. "You'll be fine, as long as you stay down for...." She looked at Owen. "How busy is she?"

"Oh, she's a ten."

Gina could've sworn she caught a slyness to Owen's smile, and her blood heated to an almost intolerable level.

"Ten?" Doctor Blithe considered her, those electric blue eyes not missing a single thing. "I can see that. So a week, Gina. You can't do much more than get up and go to the bathroom for a week."

"A week?" Gina looked back and forth between Owen and Doctor Blithe. They might as well as sentenced her to life in prison. "But we were going to go running in the morning."

"No running," Doctor Blithe said. "For at least a week. Slow walking if you have to do something." She turned to Owen. "Slow walking. No stairs."

"She lives here," Owen said. "So no stairs is just fine."

"She shouldn't be alone tonight." Doctor Blithe put her medical gear back in her bag. "Do you have family or someone you can stay with?"

Gina had no idea how to respond. Not only did she not

have family here in Getaway Bay, she didn't have family anywhere. At least not any family she cared to know about.

And friends?

"I can stay—"

"She can stay with me," Owen said, the volume of his voice almost causing an echo off the ceiling.

Gina blinked at him. "You?" He'd told her all about his two boys, and she wondered how he'd explain her sudden presence at their house.

"I make killer pancakes." He smiled and nodded at Doctor Blithe, who lifted her bag and turned toward the door. Owen stepped with her and they had a whispered exchange that Gina wanted to care about, but her head felt too poundy.

She picked up another cheese stick, wondering when she'd last eaten a pancake. It had been a while, probably four years since Ian had cut and run with half of her profits.

But she'd picked herself up then, just like she had before.

The door clicked closed, and Gina looked at Owen. "I don't need a babysitter."

"Oh, of course you don't. But I don't cross Joyce Blithe. She was *my* babysitter growing up, and trust me, it's better to just do what she says." He plucked his suit jacket from the peg by the door. "I can get someone to stay with you here, if you'd like. I'm sure Jason Burnes would stay if I asked him."

The thought of having a near-stranger—even if Jason was one of her best friend's husbands—stay in her room made Gina's skin crawl.

"No, thank you."

"You can't stay alone tonight, Gina." He sounded

polished and poised, as always. But there was a tenderness to his voice that called to her soul. Or maybe she'd imagined it because she wanted to go home with him.

"Fine." She picked up another piece of cheese.

He flashed a smile and stuck his hands in his pockets. "When you're finished, we'll go. Zach made pizza pockets for dinner."

"Your sons cook?"

"Yes. Sometimes necessity is a great teacher." He hadn't told her a whole lot about his past, but she knew he was divorced, with full custody of his teenagers.

And Gina had never wanted children. She stood slowly, needing to tell him everything about herself right now.

*Now.*

She blinked, her vision blurring around the edges, and said nothing.

"You don't look so great," he said, tucking her hand in his elbow. "Let's get you home and in bed."

"Just what every woman wants to hear." She smiled at him, the action almost making her pass out.

Owen chuckled, the sound rumbling all the way down inside Gina's body. "Which part? That you don't look great, or that I'm taking you home?"

Gina couldn't keep up with the flirting, or the double-meanings, or the sarcasm. But she smiled at Owen and held on tighter so she wouldn't fall down again.

Seven days in bed sounded heavenly about now, especially if she had the handsome Owen Church as her personal nurse.

The scent of Italian meats met Gina's nose when Owen opened his front door, and a wave of nausea hit her hard.

"Guys," Owen called. "We're here."

She didn't dare let go of him, though she didn't need his kids to see her hanging on him like she couldn't hold herself up. But she honestly wasn't sure she could.

A miniature and younger version of Owen stepped around the corner, a black apron tied around his waist. "Hey, Dad." His eyes moved to Gina, and she lifted her hand in a wave.

"She fell and hit her head," Owen said. "Joyce said she couldn't be alone tonight, and she doesn't have any family on the island."

If his son thought that was true or not, Gina couldn't tell.

"Gina, this is Cooper. He's my fifteen-year-old, and apparently the one in charge of the salad tonight."

It was at that moment that Gina noticed the tongs in Cooper's hand. Another, older, boy peeked around the wall.

He had lighter hair and lighter eyes, though his skin had obviously seen a lot of sun. "Hey, Dad. Pockets will be out in four minutes." He looked at Gina and went back into the kitchen.

"You don't want to eat, right?" Owen leaned down, his mouth almost brushing her ear.

Gina just needed to lie down. "No, thank you." Her voice sounded like half of who she was.

"Let me show you where you can stay." Thankfully,

Owen didn't take her toward the kitchen, but through a doorway and into an obvious guest bedroom.

"Bathroom here, Gina. I'm going to eat with the boys and come check on you." He gazed down at her with so many emotions in his expression that Gina couldn't separate them all.

He cradled her face, almost like he'd kiss her again, and then dropped his hand. "If you tell me what you need, I'll go get it."

Gina nodded, not quite sure what he meant. It wasn't until he closed the door behind him and she collapsed on the comfortable queen bed that she realized she had nothing. No toothbrush. No pajamas. Nothing.

# FOUR

OWEN ENJOYED his late dinner with his sons, as Zach had gotten quite good at making pizza pockets, steak and potatoes, and grilled shrimp.

"So," he said. "Have you heard anything about the University of Hawaii?"

"The deadline was three weeks ago, Dad." Zach could've added an eye roll and it would've fit the tone perfectly.

"I know," Owen said, spearing another forkful of salad and trying not to think about Gina only a couple of walls away. "But they send scholarship letters pretty quickly."

"If you get one." Zach took an overly large bite of his pizza pocket, a clear indication that he wanted the conversation to move on to something else.

"You'll get one," Owen said, totally not moving on to something else. "Your GPA and test scores were great."

"He wants to go to UCLA," Cooper said nonchalantly, but the words caused Owen to choke.

He wiped his face with his napkin, sure some bits of pizza had gotten on his chin. "What? UCLA?"

"Cooper," Zach growled.

"I didn't even know you'd applied to UCLA," Owen said, refusing to raise his voice, lower it, or otherwise act like he cared. But UCLA? That was across the ocean. And Owen couldn't just jaunt over to see his son during his first year of college if he went to school in California.

Panic built beneath his breastbone, especially when Zach didn't say anything.

"I did apply," he finally said. "I used my own money for the application."

"You didn't need to do that," Owen said in his most political voice, the one he used on patrons at the hotel who were angry about something. "I would've paid for it."

"I know that, Dad." Zach speared his younger brother with another look, but Owen was glad Cooper had said something.

"What's at UCLA?" he asked.

"Nothing," Zach said. "It's just different. It's...."

"Not here." Owen knew what Zach wanted, and he probably wouldn't find it in Hawaii, no matter how much he wanted him to.

He'd felt the pull to leave Getaway Bay before, and he had. Just a hop, skip, and jump over to another island was all. He'd sold a lot of real estate in Maui and had come back to Getaway Bay when Linda was pregnant with Zach.

"It's not that, Dad."

"I know what it is." Owen took another bite and smiled

at his son, though he felt the sadness taking root at the back of his heart.

"What are you planning to study?" he asked, glad his voice didn't hitch. He'd had so much practice concealing how he really felt, first with his wealthy real estate clients, then with almost everyone he dealt with at Sweet Breeze, and now with Gina.

The last thought surprised him. He didn't want to hide how he felt about her, and maybe now that he'd kissed her—albeit just a peck—and held her hand....

*That wasn't hand holding,* he told himself, and he knew it. She wasn't in her right mind, and he wondered if she was if she'd tell him about her foster families or let him caress her face and flirt with her about taking her home and putting her to bed.

"Basketball tomorrow at four," he said, maybe a touch too brightly. "Right, Coop?"

His younger son grinned at him. "Right, Dad. And I have a surprise for you."

"Oh, yeah?"

"He's starting at guard," Zach said, and Cooper yelled, "Hey! You jerk."

"You told my news about UCLA."

Cooper tossed a piece of lettuce at Zach, and Owen held up one hand.

"Guys, come on."

"Only because you've been too chicken to talk to Dad about it for months." Cooper glared, his face bright red. "You had no right to tell him."

Zach shrugged like it was no big deal, but Owen knew the fury was there, simply simmering below the surface. Zach might look more like Linda, but he had Owen's personality, his ability to take things and stuff them way down deep until they were like a cancer, eating at him. Then he'd explode.

"It's fine, Coop," he said, keeping one eye on Zach and one on Cooper. "Starting guard, huh? That's amazing. What happened to Bryce?"

"Nothing," Cooper said, settling back to normal though he didn't put anything else in his mouth. "I just beat him for the spot this game. Coach wants to see how it goes."

Pride welled within Owen, and he grinned at his sons. "Great news. Can you be there, Zach, or do you have to work?"

He looked at Owen and then Cooper. "I'll be there."

Since that was his way of apologizing, Owen didn't press the issue and they finished dinner.

"I'm going to go check on Gina," he said once the left-over pizza pockets had been wrapped in foil and put in the fridge.

"Who is she again?" Zach asked.

"She's doing the closets at the hotel," Owen said. "She fell on the job today and hit her head." He omitted the part where he'd acted like the one with a traumatic brain injury and had kissed her while she was down. "And Joyce said she shouldn't be alone."

"So she's a co-worker."

"Kind of." Owen studied his son. "What if she wasn't?"

Zach blinked, clearly not expecting this conversation. "I don't know."

Owen didn't either, so he just tossed the washcloth back in sink and said, "I'll be in my office after I see how she's doing. If you've got homework, get it done."

He left the boys in the kitchen and went back to the front of the house, where the guest bedroom sat across the hall from the office, a bathroom between them. He'd installed a door there too, almost making a little suite for himself since Zach often brought friends over and their electric guitars were loud.

No light shone under the crack in the door, but he knew Gina didn't have anything for her stay here. He hadn't had female articles of clothing in the house for a decade. What was her plan? Sleep in her clothes? Finger-brush her teeth?

He knocked, the proper gentleman in him not allowing such meager living when the modern necessities were five minutes away. "Gina?"

She didn't answer, and he tried the doorknob to find it unlocked. "Gina? It's Owen. Can I come in?"

"Yeah." Her voice sounded tinny and far away, and Owen wondered if when Joyce said she shouldn't be alone, she meant it literally.

Owen entered the room, the only light coming from the hallway behind him. His eyes took precious moments to adjust, and then he found Gina sitting up in bed, the comforter tucked around her legs.

"Do you need me to run and grab you a toothbrush or something?" he asked, pausing several feet from her.

Their eyes met, and Owen felt that invisible charge, that strong tether, form between them again, pulling against his resolve to keep his distance.

"A toothbrush would be nice." She smiled, but it didn't contain nearly the wattage it usually did.

"And you eat bananas for breakfast," he said. "I remember that. Pajamas?"

She shook her head. "I can sleep in my clothes."

"I can grab something at the drugstore," he said, the very idea of sleeping in jeans repulsive to him. "Even a big T-shirt or something." He did not allow his mind to travel down any forbidden paths.

"If you want to."

"How's your head?"

"It hurts."

He checked his watch. "You can take some more painkillers in about an hour, if we start rotating them."

She nodded, wincing with pain, and his heart twitched in his chest to *help her*. Help her somehow.

"What time is it?" she asked.

"Almost eight-thirty."

"So I have to stay awake until nine-thirty?"

"I can bring them in to you," he said. "I rarely sleep more than four or five hours at night."

Her eyes drifted closed, and she looked absolutely angelic lying there. "That's not healthy, you know."

He chuckled, insane fantasies floating around inside his mind. "Probably not. But someone keeps insisting I go running at five-thirty in the morning." And he'd gladly given up the extra hour of sleep he usually got.

"It's too hot otherwise," she said, a smile curving those full lips.

"You should be here in the summer." He meant it as a

joke, but he suddenly didn't feel jovial. "Will you be here this summer?" He took a step toward her but stalled when she opened her eyes.

"Yeah, of course. The job at Sweet Breeze goes through October. Right?"

"Oh, yeah, right." But what about after that? What about next summer? He kept those questions silent and fell back a step. "I'll go grab you what you need." He turned to leave.

"Owen?"

He spun back toward her. "Yeah?"

"Can I have some chocolate too? Whenever I was really sick, my foster mom at my last house, the one where I graduated from high school, she'd bring me chocolate." That smile drifted across her face again. "She said it cured everything."

"What kind?" he asked, wanting to make sure he got this right for her. "Dark? Sea salt? Caramel?"

"Whatever looks good."

He didn't like that answer, but he accepted it. He'd noticed over the weeks of his friendship with Gina that she was not a picky eater. She did not like to make decisions about what to order or make distinctions as to which kind of chocolate was best.

He pulled the door closed behind him, texted the boys that he was going to the store and they could request one treat each, and got behind the wheel of his car.

As he drove through the Hawaiian night, he realized that Gina probably had very few choices in her life growing up. She didn't get to decide what kind of chocolate her foster mom brought her. She took what was offered or went without.

His heart, usually so full on a night with a full moon such as tonight, with the ocean lapping against the shore, felt like someone had frozen it in liquid nitrogen and then shattered it.

He wanted to do something—be someone good—for Gina. Insane curiosity crawled through him at how she'd gotten to where she was.

He knew she met with the Nine-0 Club, and he knew how meticulously Fisher researched those members. So Gina was definitely a billionaire.

The real question that plagued Owen as he picked out a red toothbrush and a long nightshirt that said "Yeti for bed" on it with a big white creature on the front was: Did she want a boyfriend?

If he offered, would she take him?

# FIVE

GINA WAS aware of Owen coming in and out, saying something...she couldn't remember, and then waking sometime in the middle of the night to the soft, steady breathing of another human being nearby.

She hadn't had that sound in her bedroom since her freshman year of college. After that, she'd decided she wanted to live on her own, and she'd picked up extra hours on any job she could find to make it happen.

After all, she's had enough of sleeping two or three or even sometimes four to a bedroom.

Her heart pounded out a syncopated rhythm as she tried to figure out what had happened. Her head hurt so bad tears came to her eyes. She closed them, because the pain lessened when she wasn't trying to search through the darkness for things she couldn't see anyway.

The smell of musky cologne and wilderness hit her, and she remembered where she was.

"Owen?"

As if her voice had reached right into his slumber and awakened him, he said, "Yeah? You okay? What do you need?"

His fingers, cool as ice and filled with relief, trailed over her eyebrows.

"My head hurts."

"You wouldn't wake up for your last dose. Let me get you a drink." Owen moved and the door opened, letting in a rectangle of light, which also pierced Gina's eyes with pain.

She groaned, rolled away from the door, and covered her eyes with her arm.

"Here you go." Owen touched her elbow and she tried to sit up. She managed to do it without crying out, and she took the pills from him.

"I can take all of these?"

"I called Joyce myself." Owen supervised while she swallowed the pills and took the glass from her. "Is it okay I'm in here?" he asked. "I was really worried about you."

Gina shivered despite the warmth flowing through her. "It's fine." She didn't really want to be alone, which was a very strange sensation for her.

"You should be good until morning," he said, retreating and putting the glass on the nightstand before he settled back into the armchair only half a dozen feet from her.

She slid down the pillows to go back to sleep, but the unconsciousness didn't claim her the way she hoped it would.

Owen's breathing didn't even either, and she finally rolled toward him, the silver light from the moon illuminating his face and making him twice as gorgeous as Gina already thought he was.

"Are you still awake?" she asked, her voice barely reaching her own ears.

"I am." Only Owen Church would be so formal at four o'clock in the morning.

"Have you already gotten your four hours of sleep?"

He chuckled, and apparently that was her answer, because he didn't say anything else. Gina enjoyed the silence, glad she didn't have to fill it.

"It's nice here," she said.

"Yeah? How so?"

"I don't feel any awkwardness."

Owen's dark eyes glinted in the soft moonlight. "You've had a lot of awkward silences?"

"A fair few, yes," She closed her eyes. "What about you?"

"A couple."

"Tell me about one."

"When I found out my wife was cheating on me," he said, causing Gina's eyes to fly open.

Her heart skipped a couple of beats and then settled into its normal pulse. "What?"

"It wasn't pleasant. The silence or the conversation that followed it."

"How long ago was that?"

"Almost ten years now." He pushed his breath out. "She's somewhere in France, I think. We don't really keep in touch."

He didn't sound too terribly upset, but Gina knew how

deep wounds like that cut. Owen didn't say anything else, and Gina wasn't sure where to take the conversation next.

She wasn't particularly good at carrying a conversation to begin with, because in most of the homes where she'd lived, speaking was frowned upon.

She once again wanted to let him in, but she didn't know how. Gina closed her eyes again, letting the swish of air through the vents lull her toward peace and slumber.

The next time she woke, Owen wasn't in the room but the sun had come up and painted the furniture and walls in golden light.

Her head ached on a low level, something she worked with on a regular basis.

She ran her fingers through her hair, in dire need of a shower and a hot cup of coffee.

Knowing Owen, even the little that she did, he'd probably have a dozen flavors of creamer—and he'd probably mix them all together.

She put her legs over the edge of the bed and tested her weight on her feet. So far, so good. She made it into the bathroom to find bottles of shampoo and conditioner on the counter, along with a loofa with a tag still on it attached to a bottle of body wash. A stack of towels sat behind them, and Gina ran her fingertips along the edge of the towels, struck by the care Owen took with everything.

With his boys. With the hotel. With simple things like shampoo and painkillers. With her.

Her phone rang in the other room, and she turned away from the perfection of Owen Church to answer it.

"Stacey, hi." Her voice sounded a bit rusty and crackly along the edges.

"You were hurt at work?"

Of course she'd know. She was married to Owen's best friend. "I hit my head. I'm feeling ten times better than last night." Or even a few hours ago.

She noticed a note under the edge of her water glass. It read *Take four more of these when you wake up, there are towels in the bathroom, and there's coffee brewing. –Owen*

She spun away from his handwriting—maybe the only negative thing about him, what with those weird slants that were barely readable—expecting to see Owen standing there with a hot cup of the liquid caffeine she needed so badly.

But Owen wasn't there.

It seemed like all of her senses suddenly came to life, because she definitely smelled the coffee, like a hint of deliciousness on the air.

"Well, I just heard, and I told Fisher I'd find out."

Gina startled at Stacey's voice through her phone. "Right. Well, I'm okay. Some doctor of Owen's said I have to stay down for a week, and she didn't want me being alone last night."

"Where are you then?" Stacey sounded concerned and curious, and Gina kicked herself for saying anything.

"Oh, uh, Owen's."

"You stayed with Owen?" She practically yelled the question, which hurt Gina's head considerably.

"Just in his guest room. I was pretty out of it. But I'm feeling much better," she tacked on quickly. "Really, I am."

"Well enough to sit on the beach for an hour?"

She remembered enough from last night to know she didn't have a car here at Owen's. He always came to pick her up for their run, so she wasn't even sure where he lived.

"I don't have a car here," she said. "And I'm not even sure where Owen lives." She went to the doorway that led to the rest of the house, wondering if all the Church men had left.

Nothing moved in the house, and she padded down the hall into the kitchen, which shared space with the dining room and a living room. A computer sat on a coffee table, and the brightly colored sticker told her it wasn't Owen's.

Stacey laughed. "Well, I know where Owen lives, and I can come get you."

"I'm not supposed to do anything too strenuous," she said.

"It's lying on the beach," Stacey said. "I'll be there around ten-thirty, okay? You can tell us all about you and your *fabulous* running partner." She giggled and hung up before Gina could say she wasn't up for talking.

It didn't really matter at the Beach Club if she talked or not. So she usually didn't. Lexie had had enough news for all of them for a while, and Gina enjoyed getting to know the other women. She just didn't want to say anything about herself.

The coffee maker did indeed have coffee in it, and a sticky note on the top said, *Creamers in fridge, though you probably don't want them. Sugar on the counter.*

She poured herself a cup of coffee, using the pearly red mug sitting next to the maker. After adding a couple of spoonfuls of sugar, she sipped, sighing in relief.

Gina took the pills and texted Owen to say *You're the best host I've ever stayed with. Thank you for taking good care of me.*

He responded immediately with *How are you feeling?*

*So much better. And this coffee is amazing.* She glanced around, hoping the bag would be visible, but it wasn't. His kitchen looked like it had been professionally cleaned, though she knew Zach had made dinner the night before.

*Stay as long as you want. Nap. There's leftover pizza pockets in the fridge. Or I'll sneak away and bring you lunch.*

Gina smiled at his words, and eating lunch with him sounded wonderful. But not in yesterday's clothes and certainly not in the yeti nightshirt she currently wore.

*Stacey's coming to get me for a beach hour,* she texted. *Maybe we can eat lunch in your office and I can nap in my own place?*

*Deal. See you about noon?*

*Noon it is.*

Gina sipped her coffee, taking her time as she absorbed the calm energy in Owen's house. She thought him very practiced at keeping himself in check because of his job, but perhaps it was just his aura all the time.

No wonder she felt called toward him. Gina had not experienced much peace and calmness in her life, and she craved it.

She finished her coffee, showered, and managed to be ready in time for Stacey to pull up in a red convertible.

Gina moved slowly, the residual effects of her headache still pulsing through her with every step.

"Hey, you." Stacey grinned at her and asked, "Is that your toothbrush?"

"No, it's one Owen bought for me. I didn't want him in my place, going through my stuff."

"Oh, so you two aren't starting something."

A brief vision of that even briefer kiss flashed through Gina's mind. "Not even close."

So maybe those words lingered on the outer edge of a lie. She wanted to start something with Owen. He obviously liked her too. But there was something between them, something huge, and Gina knew exactly what it was.

Her.

She couldn't let him in, and until she did, he'd circle on the fringes, just like Davy had, and just like Ian had—until Gina had let down her defenses and let him in.

And what a disaster that had been.

"He likes you, you know." Stacey put the car in reverse and pulled out of Owen's driveway.

"Yeah, well, I like him too. We're friends."

"You know what I mean."

Gina gathered her hair into a ponytail as Stacey picked up speed. "No more talking. We're not even to the beach yet," she said. "And my head still hurts."

Stacey laughed, but she waited while Gina went upstairs at the hotel to change, and she carried everything Gina needed down to the beach. With her towel spread out, Gina stretched her arms above her head, closed her eyes, and let the sun beat down on her.

Other women arrived, but she didn't engage with them.

*He likes you, you know.*

Gina knew.

But she had no idea what to do about it.

# SIX

OWEN'S DESK looked like a bomb had gone off. At certain times of the month, there were a million little pieces of paper that needed to be signed, filed, and kept. Most of them ended up in Owen's office, needing his approval or signature.

The laundry facilities had been having a rough time keeping people on staff, and they'd just hired eight more workers. All of them needed their financial documents processed so they could get paid. Owen had to sign for that work to be done, inform the badge department that new people needed new identification, and then let the security detail know that eight more keys would be issued to the basement entrance.

Oh, and parking passes. The process to get someone hired and working for Sweet Breeze required someone full-time, but they had Owen.

He honestly didn't mind, as moving things through a

system was oddly satisfying to him. He normally didn't run late for important things like meetings or basketball games, but mealtimes were sporadic at best. So when someone knocked on his door, his first reaction was a bit of panic.

"Lunch," he said to himself.

Sure enough, Gina poked her head into the room a moment later. "Hey." She put a smile on her face, but it seemed different now. More guarded? Or less? Owen couldn't tell. "Are we eating here?" She glanced at the messy desk while Owen stood.

"No, I've got to get out of here." He rounded the desk and wanted to take her into his arms. He paused with the chair Fisher usually occupied between them.

Fisher.

Another reason Owen didn't need the knowledge of his flubbed kiss out there. Fisher would never leave him alone if he knew. "How are you feeling?" he asked, pocketing his hands and hoping his growling stomach wasn't too loud.

"So much better." She wore a pair of cutoff shorts and a tank top the color of coral. Her skin looked like she'd gotten plenty of sun that morning, even if it was technically the rainy season. She gestured to the door. "Should we go? You look busy. Or I can go grab something and bring it back. Oh, but you said you wanted to go. Okay, let's go." She turned and reached for the doorknob.

Owen sensed her nervousness, and he wasn't sure where it stemmed from. He'd appreciated their deeper conversations from yesterday, and having her meet the boys had been a big step in the right direction.

If only Owen knew what direction that was. Or how big

of a step it had been. And if it was too soon to take another one or not.

"Bagels?" he asked. "Burgers? Or salad." He knew what Gina would pick, so he wasn't surprised when she said, "The bistro."

She turned the corner and moved into the spacious lobby, leaving room for Owen at her side. He took his place there and pressed the call button for the elevator.

"I'm getting pasta today," she said. "Doesn't it feel like a pasta day?"

Owen's eyebrows lifted, and he chuckled. "It can be any kind of day you want." He thought it might be natural for him to slide his fingers into hers, tug her closer, and press his lips to her temple.

But there were about seventy pairs of eyes in the lobby— as well as the best cameras on the island—and he didn't want to broadcast his interest in the lovely Gina Jackson quite so blatantly.

The elevators had cameras too, but as he walked into the car he let his fingers brush hers casually. Their eyes met as they turned to face the closing doors, and they'd only just started to go up when she put her hand fully in his.

Owen's heart crashed against his ribs, and he couldn't help smiling like a love-struck schoolboy. "How was the beach?" he asked, wishing this elevator was the broken-down kind that barely moved.

As it was, they arrived on the fourth floor before Gina could say, "Nice. It was nice."

Owen wanted so much more than "nice." He waited

until they'd gotten a table in the corner of the bistro before saying, "Tell me about it."

Gina lifted one shoulder in a shrug, completely distracting Owen. He bounced his gaze to her bare skin there and then refocused on her face.

"It was warm," she said. "I just let the sun bake me. The other girls talked a little."

"Do you ever talk?" he asked, realizing a moment too late how his question sounded. "I mean, obviously, you talk. I just wondered what you'd talk about with them."

Gina's gaze dropped to the table and she unwrapped the silverware there like it had to be done with great care or a bomb might explode. "I don't say a lot."

Owen glanced up as a waitress appeared. She left menus and they ordered drinks before Owen could continue the conversation. "Why is that?" he asked. "You seem like an interesting person. Smart. Successful." *Beautiful.* The word echoed endlessly in his mind, and he decided to say it.

"Beautiful." He cleared his throat, wishing his water with lemon was already at the table.

Gina smiled and tucked her hair behind her ear. He wanted to know why she dyed it. Wanted to know why she'd really come to Getaway Bay. Why, why, why.

"Thank you, Owen."

The drinks arrived, and she busied herself with unwrapping a straw. Owen lifted his water right to his lips, noticing that she had not answered his question. He wondered if she would, or if he'd have to pry every little bit of information out of her.

"So I have another question for you," Owen said,

employing his general manager voice, the one he used when he wanted to soothe an upset employee or get someone to do something for him he knew they wouldn't like. "And I'd really appreciate it if you'd answer it for me. Straight up."

Something akin to panic danced across her face, but she nodded. Owen felt like someone had put a jackhammer in his stomach and switched it on high. He had no idea what to say, but somehow the words flowed from his mouth flawlessly. "Is this a date?"

Gina blinked rapidly like someone had just flicked water in her eyes. "I don't know."

"See, now that's not a straight up answer." Owen smiled and took another drink. "I'm forty-six-years-old, Gina. I don't want to play games or try to figure out some sort of signals. So I'll just say this: *I* want this to be a date. And I guess I'm wondering if you do too."

She fiddled with her discarded straw wrapper and then her hair. When she finally looked at him with those blue eyes he could fall into, he saw the answer. It was really great to hear, "Yes, I want this to be a date."

Relief rushed through him with the power of the whistling wind, and a smile popped onto his face. "Great." He reached across the table and touched her hand, calming the frantic way she worried the paper wrapper.

She stilled, lifted her eyes to his, and that great, big something that had been drawing him closer to her all these months manifested itself.

"We don't need to make a big deal of it," he said, once again finding his throat clogged with emotion. "In fact, I'd kind of like to keep it low-key while you're working at the hotel."

"Low-key?" Gina's eyes sparkled. "You mean secret."

Owen had the inexplicable urge to scratch under his collar. "Sure, secret. If that's the word you want to use. I'd like for it to…I don't know. Stay between us. I don't need Fisher on my back about it."

Gina laughed, though Owen wasn't sure what he'd said that was so funny. "What would Fisher say?" she asked.

"Oh, he's been pressuring me to start dating." Owen waved his hand like Fisher's lectures were stupid—because they were. As he'd just said, he was forty-six-years old. He didn't need to be told what to do.

Gina giggled. "He has?"

"Does that surprise you?"

"A little, yeah. At the Nine-0 meetings, he's always so…."

"Formal? Stiff?"

"Business-like."

"Oh, Fisher's big into business. He *loves* those meetings."

"There's one this afternoon."

Owen nodded as the waitress set their food down. "I'm aware. My son has a basketball game." Not that he was invited to the Nine-0 Club meetings anyway. Fisher told him all about them the next day, usually. Sometimes within the hour.

"That sounds more fun than a business meeting."

"You're not supposed to be going either." He pinned her with a look and picked up his fork. He'd ordered the pulled pork mac and cheese, while she'd opted for the boring, breadcrumb-topped version.

"I feel pretty great," she said.

"Still." He took a bite, the tangy barbecue sauce combining with the ooey gooey richness of the cheese. "You've got to try this."

"I don't like barbecue sauce."

Owen glanced up, surprise spinning through him. "You're from Texas and you don't like barbecue?"

"Miracles happen." She smirked at him and took a bite of her plain mac and cheese.

"So there's one more thing," Owen said, his pulse ricocheting through him.

"Yeah?" She stirred her food and collected another forkful of noodles.

"I want to learn something new about you every day. I know you don't like talking, and it's okay." He watched her, seeing the first signs of her retreat as her eyes shuttered off. "Honestly, it's okay. But if this is a date, and we both want it to be a date, that means we want to get to know each other a little better. Maybe see if...." He cleared his throat. The words in his mind absolutely could not be said.

"See if what?" she challenged, leaning forward. "See if that kiss in the closet can be any better?"

"Better?" Owen squeaked. Of course it was awful. He'd barely touched her before he'd jerked away.

"Maybe a better word would be longer." Gina lifted her straw to her lips as if to bring attention to them, and Owen stared at her mouth.

"I'd like it to be longer." His mouth felt so, so dry.

Gina smiled and picked up her fork again. "So you want something every day."

Owen came to his senses and sat up a little straighter. "Yeah, but it can be easy stuff. Like, today, I learned you don't like barbecue sauce."

"Okay," she said. "So what's your thing for today?"

He shook his head, his smile not quite as flirtatious now. "Oh, I'm not giving you another one."

"Another one?"

He looked right at her. "Four a.m. still counts as part of today, my friend."

Confusion puckered her eyebrows for a few seconds, and then realization lit her face. "You mean about your ex-wife."

"That's exactly what I mean." He pointed his fork at her. "And that was a *really* big one, so maybe I should get two or three things today."

He saw the fear march across her face, watched her master it, and for the first time since he'd met Gina, he thought he might just have a chance at learning all her secrets.

# SEVEN

GINA'S GUT WRITHED, but she really didn't want to ruin her chance with Owen. She couldn't even believe she *had* a chance with Owen. But there he sat, right across from her, eating that meat and pasta—with the disgusting barbecue sauce—and watching her with those sharp yet dreamy eyes.

"I don't like barbecue sauce because one of my foster dads made me eat it on everything." And it wasn't the taste she found repulsive.

Owen's eyes softened. "I'm sorry. You don't have to tell me everything."

Gina swallowed, her own mac and cheese almost tasteless because of this conversation. "But I want to."

A smile passed across his whole face, and he ducked his head as if he were fifteen and this was their first date.

Technically, it was their first date, and Gina felt just as nervous and off-kilter as Owen seemed to.

And she really didn't like that. Could she tell him that? He'd been bold with her. "So I don't like barbecue sauce, because it reminds me of him. And I went into professional organizing because I like being in control. Making things right. Straight. Perfect." All the things her life had never been. "And that's a really big one for me. I mean, my husband didn't cheat on me, but yeah." She swallowed and wished she had somewhere else to look besides in his caring eyes. "That's a big one for me."

Owen stretched out his arm and patted her hand, squeezing it. "Thank you for telling me."

Gina relaxed a little after that, and Owen turned the conversation to lighter things. Surprisingly, only forty-five minutes passed before he said, "I hate to run, but I have a ton of work to do before I head out for the basketball game. Shall I walk you up to your room?"

"Is that too public?" she asked, quite enjoying this idea of a forbidden, secret romance with the handsome general manager.

He sighed and ran his hand down his jaw, which he hadn't shaved that morning. She wondered if he didn't have time or simply forgot. She'd never seen him with facial hair and it made him look more rugged. Sexier.

"Probably." He stopped at the elevator and pushed the up button. "So I'll see you later."

"We never did talk about the new closet design."

"You're not supposed to be working."

"I can sit and talk about a blueprint as easily as I just sat and ate pasta." She grinned at him, not wanting to leave until she knew when she'd see him again. And that really spoke volumes to her about how she felt about Owen.

"We can't run in the morning," he said. "But we could get together for coffee and blueprints, I suppose."

The elevator doors closed again, the car rushing off to another floor. Owen didn't even seem to notice as he continued to talk to himself. "I have a meeting at nine, though. Our water incentive is up for renewal."

Like Gina knew what that meant, but she smiled and said, "I can meet whenever you say."

"Seven-thirty?"

Seeing as that was two hours later than she usually went running with him, she agreed, pushed the elevator button again, and rode up to her room on the eighth floor alone.

The phantom of Owen's hand against hers went with her, and she swallowed a few pills before collapsing into bed. Maybe she was a little run-down. After all, she'd showered, lain on the beach, and had lunch and she felt like she needed to sleep for days.

———

Four o'clock came, and Gina stepped off the private elevator to Fisher's penthouse. She'd spent at least twenty minutes trying to decide what to wear—because she wasn't sure which event she'd be going to. Her boring business meeting? Or to a high school basketball game?

In the end, she decided that attending a game for her boyfriend's son was anything but low key.

Then she freaked out about the word *boyfriend*. That

word running through her mind right now sent shivers down her arms and back.

Owen was not her boyfriend. They'd gone on one date—lunch, no less—and agreed to see each other for coffee the next morning. He was her friend, and without the *boy* on the front, Gina's nerves settled.

"You came." The surprise in Lexie's voice was only matched by Gina's when the other woman hugged her. Gina did not like to be touched, but she patted Lexie awkwardly and stepped back as soon as she could.

"I'm feeling better," she said. "Nothing a little nap can't fix." She added a smile, and Lexie returned it.

"How's the mutual fund business?" Gina took a bottle of water from the rows of them on the credenza. Fisher stood over by the windows, his head bent together with Marshall Robison. Ira and Gabi sat on the couch together, their fingers entwined. Gina stared openly at them while Lexie said something about her brother in New York and the rise of the technology sector.

"What about you?" Lexie asked. "How did Owen like the closet design?"

Gina jerked her attention back to Lexie. "The closet design?"

Lexie peered at her like she'd lost her mind. "Yeah, you said you two were working on something together. Bagels. Blueprints."

"Oh, right." Gina laughed lightly, but her heart was still trying to fling itself free from her body. "It's not going to work out."

"No? You two seemed so sure."

Gina honestly couldn't keep track of the conversation. Did Lexie know about her and Owen holding hands? Practically confessing their feelings. They seemed so sure of what?

Thankfully, before the silence got too awkward, Jasper stepped into the room, diverting Lexie's attention.

"Excuse me, Gina." She touched Gina's arm and moved past her, already calling, "Jasper, I need to talk to you about something."

Gina watched her go, watched the easy way she talked with Jasper like they were old friends. Which, of course, they were. It was only Gina who was new.

*Not true*, she told herself. Gabi was new too, though she fit right in with her sophisticated clothes and stylish hairstyle. Gina had never seen the woman wear anything but heels, even with jeans. Gina didn't even know all the ways she was supposed to act as a billionaire, and she wished Owen were with her.

He was polished, poised, and practiced. She was a country bumpkin who'd worked hard, gotten lucky, and refused to give up.

Even though she had money now, she still didn't know the latest fashions or how to make her hair lay flat like the celebrities did. Sure, she could hire someone, and she had in the past. But it was so hard to know who to trust these days.

"Let's gather over here," Fisher finally said just as Gina was gearing up to make her early exit. "Ira has some news out of London."

Intellectually, Gina knew she needed to expand outside the United States if she wanted to take Classy Closets to the next level. But she was barely hanging on with the business she had now.

She gathered with everyone else and listened like she knew what Ira was talking about. But she didn't understand how the economy of another country could affect her. The others seemed gravely concerned, especially Jasper, whose diamond mines and business were globally located and operated.

Gina made it through without saying anything, just like she had many, many times before. As she left the meeting, though, she wondered why she allowed herself to fade into the background.

She was smart. She could learn global economics, just like she'd learned how to interview and hire employees, set up payroll, manage a team of people.

So she'd trusted the wrong person once. Did that mean she'd never be able to trust again?

As she set her feet down the beachwalk toward The Straw, Lexie at her side, she decided that she was done letting Ian's behavior drive hers.

So he'd stolen from her. Lied to her. Left her. She hadn't been broken—and it was time to start acting like it.

"Who does your shopping?" she asked Lexie as they joined the line outside the drink stand.

Lexie looked at her, clearly flummoxed. "What?"

Gina indicated her clothes. "Your shopping. You have someone, right?"

Lexie glanced down at her outfit—a pair of black slacks, black flats, and a purple-blue blouse with white flowers splashed all over it. She was the picture of professional and approachable.

"Why? Is it that bad?"

Gina frowned. "I need some help when it comes to fashion. I thought maybe I'd hire your person."

Lexie started laughing and linked her arm through Gina's. "I don't have a person," she said. "I picked these out myself."

Gina grinned at her. "Then maybe *you'll* help me find some cute stuff."

"You want to go shopping together?" They stepped forward, and Sasha perked up.

"Shopping?" she said. "I'm in. And Tawny's been dying to go find a new formal dress. I guess Tyler's got another black tie event, and she insists she can't wear the same thing as last time."

Gina's first instinct was to back out, go alone. But she resisted it and said, "Sure. When should we go?"

Sasha looked at Maddy, the woman helping her in the stand today. "Tomorrow? You want to work again?"

"So you can go shopping?" Maddy ripped off another order and waggled the paper in front of Sasha's nose. "I guess so. I could use the extra hours since Palu didn't get a scholarship." She rolled her eyes and mumbled something in Hawaiian that Lexie laughed about.

Gina ordered the same thing she always did—the Hawaiian Rockstar, with peach, power powder, strawberries, and "rockstar" fruit—and stood off to the side. Out of the way. Not in the conversation.

So maybe it would take more than a couple of conversations for a new habit to start. As Sasha made and passed out drinks, finally getting to Gina and Lexie, Gina was just proud that she hadn't gone straight back to her room after the Nine-0 Club meeting. That she'd gone out with Lexie, talked to her, and now had a shopping trip on the horizon for tomorrow.

She wouldn't be telling Owen about that. Combined with the coffee date they had, he'd insist she should be lying down instead of shopping.

But Gina worked hard for her money, and it was about time she spent some of it.

"So," Lexie said as they meandered down the beach, back toward the bigger bay. "I wasn't at the Women's Beach Club this morning, but I heard a whisper about you and a certain general manager."

Gina shook her head and sucked on her smoothie. "Nothing to whisper about."

"You sure?" Lexie peered at her, and there was something about the woman that could see through steel. At least Gina thought so.

"He's...."

"Handsome?" Lexie supplied. "Rich? Hard-working? Seriously, there's nothing to dislike about Owen Church."

Oh, but there was. Gina just didn't want to say so out loud. "He has bad handwriting."

Lexie laughed, her feet kicking up sand as she scuffed them. "If that's his biggest flaw, then you should marry him tomorrow."

The very thought of marriage sent Gina into a tailspin, and she worked to right herself emotionally again. Lexie knew very little about her. Heck, no one knew anything about her.

"I'm not the marrying type," she said. "Or the motherly type, if you get my drift."

Lexie brushed her hair off her face. "So Owen's biggest flaw is his kids?"

"Something like that." Gina gazed out over the water, finding it tranquil, with hardly any undulation in it. But she knew better. She knew that once a person got out in the bay, the water could be choppier than could be seen from shore.

"You're an interesting person, Gina," Lexie said.

"Owen said that too." Gina looked at Lexie, knowing the other woman wanted the same thing Owen did, just on a friendship level instead of a relationship level. "He wants me to tell him all my secrets."

Familiar fear gripped Gina's stomach. "I don't know if I can."

Lexie wore a sympathetic smile that only touched her mouth. She linked her arm through Gina's and said, "One question, and then maybe a solution. You game?"

"I guess."

"Do you like Owen? Want to maybe see if you two could be together?"

"Yes." Gina could barely get the word past the lump in her throat. Zach was graduating this year. She wouldn't really have to play the domestic mother, a role she knew nothing about and didn't want to learn.

"Okay, that's a start."

"What's the solution?" Gina asked.

"You tell me all your secrets first, as practice. And then it won't be so hard when you tell Owen."

Gina thought sure Lexie was joking, but one direct look at her, and nope.

"You look like I said you'll have to swim with sharks." Lexie smiled and focused on the horizon again. "I didn't have a great childhood either. My father was an alcoholic."

Gina let the sand sift over her feet, the heat of it almost burning but not quite. She wanted this friendship, to anchor herself to something human again, to not feel so alone.

Maybe Getaway Bay and the people she'd met here were exactly what she needed.

"I grew up in the foster care system," she said. "Because my mother was a drug addict and I don't know who my father is."

"Oh, wow." Lexie's arm tightened. "I can see why you maybe don't want to tell Owen."

"I've told him that one."

"So you've already started." Lexie danced ahead of her, grinning like the Cheshire Cat.

Gina couldn't help the grin that graced her face in return. But she wasn't sure about this arrangement. Perhaps she could judge how Owen would take things based on Lexie's reactions though.

"What else have you got?" Lexie asked, and Gina shook her head, a laugh starting to rumble up from deep inside.

# EIGHT

OWEN JUMPED TO HIS FEET, yelling for his son, who'd just launched the ball from the corner of the free throw line—and hit the shot. Only fifteen seconds remained in the game, and the basket had just put Cooper's team up by one.

The two teams had been volleying back and forth for the past six minutes, and Owen wasn't sure he could handle the stress. He really wanted Cooper's first starting game to be a winner.

Beside him, Zach cheered too, something that filled Owen's heart with gladness. Zach had been acting strange the past couple of months, and Owen had attributed it to the scholarship application process, but maybe it was the UCLA secret. Or maybe something else.

But Zach seemed like himself at the moment, and when he'd had to be reminded three times to come to the game.

The crowd yelled for both sides, and the guard on the

opposing team just kept dribbling the ball. Bounce, bounce, bounce. If he got off the last shot and sank it....

Owen pressed his eyes closed, the noise swirling around him. There had to be only a few seconds left.

He opened his eyes and glanced at the clock. Four seconds. The guard shot. From his slanted position down the court, he couldn't tell if it would go in or not.

It hit the rim, bounced, hit again, and fell out.

Owen couldn't believe he could still get his feet off the ground, but he did it. He jumped and clapped Zach on the back, his face hurting from the width of his smile.

While he didn't like that one team had to lose—there could very well be a boy on the other team who'd just started for the first time and really wanted to win—Owen had learned that, in life, there were winners and losers.

His real estate career had taught him that. So had his first marriage. And his boys taught him that every day.

His pocket buzzed, and he pulled his phone out to find Fisher's name on the screen. He didn't answer it—Owen wouldn't be able to hear the call anyway—and instead sent a text. *I need ten minutes. Call you then. Okay?*

Fisher responded with *Okay. Did Coop win?*

*Yes!*

Owen put his phone away as the crowd emptied onto the floor. He managed to stay behind Zach, who'd grown an inch taller than him over the past year, and they made their way to Cooper.

"You did it!" Owen shouted, giving his son a big hug. Moments like this made his wish he could be two people: a mother and a father. His sons had never gone without, at least monetarily. But Owen knew they struggled from time to time for no reason other than their mom had abandoned them a decade ago.

Zach had quit his counseling in October, when he'd turned eighteen. Owen still made Cooper go every month, and he didn't complain about it—yet.

He held Cooper tighter for maybe a moment longer than necessary and then released him to Zach, who also hugged him.

"Celebratory dinner," he said. "Wherever you want."

"I've gotta do the end-game stuff," Cooper said.

"Yeah, of course. We'll wait." Owen refused to think about the towers of work he'd left on his desk. It would still be there tomorrow, barring a volcanic eruption or a huge tropical storm. And he'd have heard of those if they were about to happen.

"Half an hour," Cooper said, grinning for all he was worth as the coach called for him to join the team.

The adrenaline wore off and Owen dialed Fisher to find out what his boss needed. "Hey," he said. "What's up?"

"Are you coming back tonight?" Fisher asked.

"Not for a while. Gonna go out with the boys to celebrate. Cooper hit the winning shot."

"That's great," Fisher said, pure sincerity in his voice. "So I'll just see you tomorrow."

"I might run over after," Owen said. "Depends on how late we go." At five-thirty on an almost weekend, the dinner crowds could be big. It wasn't unusual for him to work late —sometimes as late as nine or ten.

Cooper chose the best burger joint on the island, but it

wasn't in Getaway Bay. Around the curve sat a dude ranch, with cattle and cowboys and everything. And their hamburgers were the best in the United States, but being in Hawaii, they didn't get the recognition they deserved.

Owen grinned as he watched his son eat the fried dill pickle burger and his beer-battered French fries. Zach talked a lot, and Owen committed these joyful, fun moments to his memory.

The band finished their set, and Owen said, "Should we go? Who has homework?"

By the looks on his sons' faces, Owen knew they both did. Neither spoke. He chuckled, and said, "I have to go back to the hotel. You guys want to grab your stuff and come over and work on it in my office? Or should I drop you at home?"

"I'll come over," Cooper said.

"Me too." Zach shoved his phone in his back pocket and smiled at his dad.

So Owen drove all the way back around the island so his boys could get their backpacks, and then they went back to Sweet Breeze.

When he opened the door to his office, he found Fisher sitting at his desk as if the man had expected Owen to walk in at any moment.

"Fisher." Surprise colored Owen's voice. "How long have you been here?" He waited for Cooper and Zach to enter and everyone exchanged hellos.

"I have something for you." Fisher grinned at Cooper. "I heard you hit the winning shot today." Fisher tucked his hands in his pockets but he wore a wolfish grin that meant

Cooper was about to get an outrageous gift from the billionaire.

Owen had stopped protesting and had chosen to spend his time and energy lecturing the boys to be grateful, say thank you and mean it, and not let anything inflate their egos.

Zach took his backpack to the couch against the wall and sat down while Cooper accepted an envelope from Fisher.

"What's this, Mister DuPont?" Cooper flipped it over and over.

"Open it and see." Fisher tossed a look at Owen, who raised his eyebrows.

Cooper ripped the flap and pulled out a pair of tickets. "The Blues Street Boys." He laughed, his entire countenance brightening. "Thank you, Fisher." He hugged the man as they both chuckled.

"I have it on very good authority that they're your favorite band."

"They are," Cooper said, looking at Owen. "Did you tell him that?"

"I did not." Owen moved around the desk, wondering what Fisher had disturbed and how long he'd been there.

"Who did then?"

"Stacey told me," Fisher said, grinning. "The woman has a way of learning things. I don't try to understand anymore."

"Stacey takes the boys to lunch once a month," Owen said as he sat down. "Coop probably told her then."

"I don't remember," Cooper said, but Zach said, "Yeah,

you were going on about them coming to the island, to that ranch where we just ate."

"That was months ago." Cooper looked at the tickets. "They've been sold out forever."

"Well, sometimes money can buy things that are sold out." Fisher grinned and said, "Can I steal your dad for a few minutes?"

Owen didn't like the sound of that, especially with the piles of paperwork he wanted gone from his desk by morning. But he stood anyway. "The boys have homework. Get started, guys. We'll be back in a minute."

Fisher led the way into the hall, and they moved down to Fisher's office. Owen didn't like how Fisher didn't start talking right away, but waited until they were both inside with the door closed.

So something personal. Owen prepared himself to deny everything.

"So." Fisher groaned as he sank into the leather armchair in the corner of the room. His desk was pristine, as Fisher didn't actually do much work here. If there was something to be done, he brought it to Owen's office.

Owen sat in the chair across from him. "So."

"Stacey told me you housed Gina Jackson at your home last night."

"I did." Owen kept his face impassive, blank, his voice even. "She hit her head in the suite on the fifth floor. Joyce said she shouldn't be alone, and she doesn't have any family on the island." Owen blinked and took a moment to breathe. "So it was either have her stay in the guest bedroom, or stay with her in the standard room on the eighth floor." He raised his eyebrows, a silent question as to which Fisher would've had him do.

"I know you like Gina Jackson." Fisher wore a sly smile, but Owen shook his head.

"We run together. Work together. We're friends." Owen swallowed and fought the urge to fiddle with the knot of his tie. "That's all."

"You eat out a lot together."

"So what? You eat out with Tyler and Jasper and a scad of other people." Owen shook his head. "We review blue-prints over bagels and juice. It's not a date."

He thought about the lunch earlier that day that they absolutely had defined as a date, but Fisher would be a beast if he knew that.

"She's a beautiful woman."

"Is this what you called me about?" Owen rolled his eyes. "I have work to do, Fisher. I didn't bring the boys over so you could lecture me about dating. Again."

Fisher laughed and held up his hands in surrender. "All right. I just…I think Cooper and Zach would be open to you dating."

Fisher was a brilliant man. Keen, and observant, and kind. But he hadn't raised two sons by himself, nor did he completely understand the dynamics of a family and adding someone new to it after such a long period of time.

"When I meet someone I'm interested in," Owen said as he stood. "I'll talk to the boys about it. Until then…." He shrugged, glad he didn't sound like he'd just fibbed.

Because he *had* met someone he was interested in, but he

rather liked the idea of keeping the budding relationship a secret—from his boys and from everyone else.

*Besides,* he thought as he returned to his office and got back to work. *Things with Gina are going to go very slowly.* And he didn't need Fisher or Stacey asking him about her every time he saw them.

# NINE

GINA WENT to bed with a headache but woke feeling like she'd been reborn. Hopefully Doctor Blithe would be proven wrong, and Gina would feel better long before a week passed.

She'd enjoyed her afternoon with Lexie and had gone to bed early, thoughts of Owen swirling through her mind strong enough to influence her dreams.

She smiled as she thought about kissing him but frowned when she realized how much she'd have to reveal to get to that point.

She hadn't told Lexie much more about her life in the foster care system, and while she knew it had formed a large part of who she was, she also knew it didn't define her.

Since she had a breakfast date with Owen and a full afternoon of shopping ahead, Gina got out of bed and into the shower.

The nagging thought that she needed to find somewhere to live on the island wouldn't leave her. Neither would the idea that she needed to find a therapist here too. She'd had a great one in Texas, and he'd helped her a lot. Maybe if she saw someone here, she wouldn't mess things up with Owen.

Because of the time difference, when she got out of the shower, she was able to get the receptionist at her therapist's office in Dallas.

"Hello, Felicia. It's Gina Jackson."

"Gina!" She sounded so happy to hear from her. "We haven't seen you in so long."

"I'm working in Hawaii right now." Gina chuckled. "And I'm actually wondering if I can get a recommendation for someone here."

"Oh, are you moving there permanently?"

"Possibly," Gina said, unable to commit.

"Let me talk to Doctor Johns and I'll give you a call back."

"Thanks, Felicia." Gina hung up, feeling like she'd accomplished a day's worth of work with a single phone call.

She dressed, dried her hair and let it fall over her shoulders however it wanted, and put on mascara and lip gloss. She'd scrape her hair into a ponytail by the time breakfast ended, but she at least wanted to attempt to wear her hair down.

With several minutes to spare before she needed to head downstairs, she decided she should probably check in with her office manager at the Classy Closets headquarters in Dallas.

"Toni," she said when the woman answered. "I've been getting your weekly emails. Things going okay?"

"Just fine, ma'am." Toni had worked for Gina from the beginning of the company—she'd been Gina's first employee —but she still called everyone "sir" or "ma'am." Claimed it was because of the Southern manners her momma had beat into her.

"Tell me about the Hamilton job. It got done on time. Nicki was satisfied?" Nicki Hamilton had hired Gina to do all the closets in her home, one at a time, and she'd referred over a dozen people to Classy Closets over the years.

"All done. Filled out the online survey with rave reviews, as usual."

"Good, good." Gina had left in the middle of Nicki's job, and while she'd visited with the woman before leaving for Getaway Bay, Gina had carried a bit of guilt at not staying to finish the job.

"And Mariah quit?"

"Her last day is next Friday, yes."

"Do we have anyone to take her place?"

"You usually do all the hiring, ma'am. I did ask you about it in last week's email."

Gina closed her eyes, her mind a little slower than it normally was. "You're right. You did." She took in a big lungful of air and released it. "Well, I'm afraid I'm not going to be back for months." She let the words hang there. She trusted Toni. "Toni, who would be a good general manager?" She thought of Owen and the complete trust between him and Fisher DuPont. She needed an Owen for her business, the way she'd once used Ian.

"Wait," Gina said. "Do you want to be the general manager? You'd do the hiring, the payroll, all that kind of stuff. We could move someone into your job of managing the schedule, the jobs, the reports...." Gina felt a ray of hope cut through her.

It felt like a huge step to be hiring someone to replace Ian. Because it wasn't a simple hiring. It was Gina placing her utmost trust in a person, something that scared her beyond reason. She swallowed, waiting for Toni to say something.

"Well, Gina," Toni said, and Gina knew she was serious when she used her name and not *ma'am*.

Gina pulled in a breath and held it. "You've been with me forever," she said. "You know what happened with Ian."

"I do," Toni said. "And I'd love to be your general manager."

"Yeah?" Gina laughed, the sound quite nervous. "That's great."

"I know what this means," Toni said.

Gina sobered. "Yeah, I know you do." A moment passed and though the two women were thousands of miles apart, Gina felt a connection to Toni. "I'll get the paperwork over to you by tonight." She cleared her throat. "And you can hire someone to be a designer to replace Mariah, and someone to take your job." Gina smiled just thinking about what she'd done. Not only had she allowed herself to trust someone again, she was making it so she could stay in Getaway Bay permanently.

But Toni didn't need to know that right now. It was

enough that the job at Sweet Breeze would take months and months, so someone was needed to make sure operations in Dallas kept going. Simple as that.

"I'll keep you informed, ma'am," Toni said, and Gina said goodbye, now late to meet Owen for coffee.

She hurried to the elevator and once in the lobby, found him loitering near the check-in desk with Jason Burnes.

As soon as he saw her, he nodded to Jason and left the counter in favor of joining her. "Sorry I'm late," she said. "I had to call Dallas."

Owen didn't touch her and the expression on his face didn't show any emotion. "How are things in the company?"

"Great." She grinned up at him, wanting to lace her fingers through his, pull him closer so she could smell his woodsy cologne, and tell him everything. "I hired a general manager to take care of things there."

Owen's eyebrows lifted. "Oh?"

"It's a big step for me," she said, swallowing back her fear. She hadn't run anything past Lexie yet, but she wasn't sure she needed to. "See, I used to have a partner."

They started to walk at a leisurely pace toward the exit, plenty of proper distance between them.

"His name was Ian," Gina said, the name bitter on her tongue. "He...stole half of my clients, my license to the design software I'd paid thousands to obtain, and started his own competing company."

A hiss leaked from Owen's mouth. "That's terrible. Did you get your license back?"

"I did, but it cost a lot in legal fees. And...I lost the ability to trust people for a while."

Owen nodded to the valet, who left to get his car. His fingers brushed Gina's, but he didn't grab hold of her hand the way she wanted. "I understand that. You should know I haven't dated since Linda left me."

Their eyes locked and every muscle cell in her body melted. "So we're both trying something new." She ran her fingers down the side of his face. "I kinda liked you with a beard."

She dropped her hand like his jaw had caught fire when his car came around the corner. She wanted to spring back a few steps to put more distance between them, but forced herself to do it more casually, almost like she was moving to step around the car as it came to a stop.

"Thank you, Sterling," Owen said, his voice as smooth and perfect as ever. He ducked behind the wheel, and Gina joined him in the passenger seat.

"So, coffee or do you want a full breakfast?" he asked as he put the car in drive.

"A full breakfast," she said, knowing that Owen would rather eat than drink first thing in the morning. "I know you like that place over on Tiki Road."

"The Broken Yolk." Owen grinned. "Yes."

"How was Cooper's game?" she asked, and Owen's smile widened.

"He won. Made the game-winning shot, too."

"That's great." Gina hugged her arms around herself, not wanting to think about trying to step into those boys' lives and be something she had no idea how to be. Be something she'd never *wanted* to be.

Owen said nothing more, and the gentle pressure of his hand on the small of her back as he guided her into the breakfast bar made sparks race through her bloodstream.

They waited for a table, as this Friday morning seemed to be quite busy. Once the hostess had taken them back, Owen seemed to relax.

"You look a little tired," she said.

"I had a lot of work to catch up on after the game." He yawned, actually yawned, and Gina had never seen him do that before.

"Do you ever take a day off?" she asked, a wild idea occurring to her. "Like an entire day, where you don't work, even remotely?"

He looked at her, a wariness to his gaze she actually liked. She was so used to him knowing her every move— heck, five moves ahead—that she felt like maybe she had him cornered this time.

"Sometimes," he said coolly.

"Liar." She laughed. "I'd like to know the last time you took a day off."

"I don't know the exact date."

Gina tossed her hair over her shoulder and laughed again. "Since I'm supposed to be taking it easy, and you need a day off, I was wondering if you wanted to go snorkeling with me. I've never been, and I heard there's this great cove around the island by that dude ranch?" She glanced up as a waitress arrived. "Do you snorkel?"

He didn't answer right away, instead ordering his coffee full of creamers and caramel and looking at her.

She ordered black coffee and the waitress left.

"I've been snorkeling," he said. "I grew up in Getaway Bay."

"So you have your own gear?"

"I haven't been in years."

Gina lifted one shoulder, a coyness pulling through her she hoped showed on her face. "So I'll hire someone to take me."

Owen looked at the menu when he said, "I'll take you. It's not hard."

"I don't have gear."

"We'll go buy you some." He glanced up. "When do you want to go?"

"Sunday? Can you take Sunday off?"

Owen lifted his chin. "I can, sure. I'll just need to talk to Fisher."

Gina leaned her elbows on the table. "Ooh, what will you tell him?"

"That I'm taking the day off with the boys. They love snorkeling."

Gina's heart beat too hard. "Maybe I'll be feeling better by then. Maybe we should just work on the closets." After all, this injury had set them back a week already.

The waitress arrived with their coffee and asked, "Are you ready to order?"

"Yes, I'll have the BELT," Gina practically yelled. She'd probably take two bites and switch to coffee, but then Owen wouldn't feel like she'd suggested breakfast simply for him.

"And I'll have the western omelet, with avocado and some of that pico de gallo. And the kielbasa."

Gina's worst nightmare was a bunch of vegetables, meats, and cheeses mixed into eggs, but she simply smiled as she handed the menu back to the waitress.

Owen studied her once they were alone again. "Tell me why you don't want to go snorkeling with me and my family."

"It's not that I don't," Gina said, aware of how false her voice sounded. "I just thought we were keeping this low key."

Owen sipped his coffee without looking away from her. "But not from them. I don't…I can't do that to them."

"I don't want to be a mother," she blurted out. Her eyes widened as her pulse thundered.

Owen blinked at her and couldn't seem to come up with anything to say. The chatter of people around them, the clinking of silverware against dishes, filled the air as Gina's horror and disbelief continued to build.

"I'm sorry," she said at the same time Owen said, "We're a package, Gina. I'd be interested to know why you don't want to be a mother, but I'm afraid that my boys come with me." He lifted his chin, a dark glint entering his eyes. "I understand if you don't want to pursue anything with me." He leaned forward. "But my sons are deal-breakers. They will always come first for me."

Gina nodded, said, "Of course," and tried to think of how to fix, well, herself. She couldn't come up with anything, and Owen's intensity dropped a few notches so that by the time their food came, he was able to say something about the best place to buy snorkeling gear.

But Gina felt near tears, so that when her phone rang and she saw the number to her therapist's office in Dallas, she said, "I have to take this. Excuse me," and all but ran from the table. And Owen.

# TEN

OWEN FINISHED BREAKFAST BY HIMSELF, noting that Gina had taken exactly three bites of her bacon, egg, lettuce, and tomato sandwich before scurrying away with her phone at her ear.

He sighed. He probably shouldn't have been so emphatic about how he and his sons were a package deal, but he'd felt like he needed to be. In that moment, with her pure panic etched in her eyes, he needed her to know that he wasn't going to sneak around on Zach and Cooper. He'd meant he didn't need everyone—his boss, his friends, and his employees at Sweet Breeze—knowing he was sweet on the closet designer he'd hired.

That was all.

True, Cooper and Zach spent a fair amount of time with Stacey and Fisher, but Owen felt confident he could have a frank conversation with his boys about his relationship with Gina, when they were ready to reveal it.

And if she wanted him to take a day off work and spend it with her, she had to know that meant they had to tell his sons about them.

"Well, you got that point across." He took another bite of his omelet, but he could barely swallow it.

He set his fork down and finished his coffee. Still, Gina had not returned. He picked up his phone and found a half-dozen messages for three different people. None of them were Gina.

He ignored the work-related texts and found Gina's thread. Instead of texting, he called her, finding that sometimes things were more easily worked out with words rather than letters.

"Hey," he said when she answered. "Please come back inside. I don't care if we don't tell Zach and Cooper about us right away. Honestly, I don't. I was simply saying that if we're going to do more than a few meals that can be interpreted as us dating, that I'd want to tell them."

"Okay."

"But I'll wait as long as you want. I'm fine with coffee in the morning, and running when you're back up for it, and... waiting." He swallowed, telling himself to stop talking.

"Okay."

"Where are you?" He held up one finger for the waitress who had just arrived. "Should I have your food boxed?"

"No." Her voice sounded in his ear and behind him. He twisted to find her almost back to the table and he hung up his phone.

She slid into the seat across from him, her face carrying a healthy blush that only made her more attractive.

Gina didn't touch her sandwich, instead going for the coffee. "So maybe snorkeling is down the road," she said, her voice a tone of forced casualness Owen didn't particularly like.

"I will always have two sons," he said, reaching across the table and placing his hands around hers as she curled them around her coffee cup. "But that doesn't mean you'll be their mother."

He struggled to find the right words. "As I've said, I've never dated. So it'll be brand new for all of us when we finally tell them. But it doesn't have to be on Sunday."

She nodded, but Owen still saw the flicker of fear in her face.

"Maybe you could tell me a bit about why you don't want to be a mother," he said gently, pulling his hands back.

She flinched but turned her hand to grip his instead of letting him pull away. Satisfaction flowed through Owen, and he really enjoyed holding Gina's hand.

She cleared her throat. "That call was from my therapist's office in Dallas."

Owen masked his emotions and merely nodded.

"I asked them for a reference for someone here. I haven't gone for a while, and I need to."

"Of course." Owen believed in talking to a professional. "My boys go. Well, Cooper still does. I told Zach he could stop when he turned eighteen, and he did. I wish he'd still go, but." Owen lifted one shoulder in a shrug. "He's an adult now. He gets to decide."

"Have you ever gone?"

"For a while, after the divorce. But not for years now."

Not since starting at Sweet Breeze, actually, when Fisher had become better at listening to Owen than the doctor he paid. "I'm glad you're going. Who are you seeing?"

"A woman named Lucinda White."

"Oh, she's in the same building where Cooper goes." Owen put a smile on his face he hoped was gentle, encouraging, and soft. "You'll have to tell me how it goes."

Gina met his eye, naked worry in hers. "All right." She drew in a deep breath and seemed to cast off the cobwebs from her soul. "Now can we *please* go back to the hotel and do some work? I don't know what I'm supposed to do with myself all day."

Owen laughed and signaled the waitress that they were ready to go.

———

They did not go snorkeling on Sunday. Gina seemed back to her regular, vibrant self—at least inside the closets. He had his regular work to do, but he managed to sneak away every day and see what she was doing in the apartment on the fifth floor.

She told him about her lack of motherly role models and that she didn't want to do to any child what had been done to her. Owen understood why she felt that way, he did. But he didn't know how to tell her that becoming a mother didn't make a person neglectful or bad. The drugs had done that to her mother, and Gina didn't do drugs.

He'd said nothing, choosing instead to listen to her and

be there for her, hold her hand, and ask her what she needed.

A week passed before she texted to say, *I'm dying to run tomorrow. You up for it?*

He couldn't say yes fast enough, and they made plans for their meeting at six o'clock in the lobby. He'd promised her he didn't need to tell Zach and Cooper about their relationship until she was ready, but that meant they had to keep doing what they'd done before that lunch date that had changed the landscape of their friendship.

She'd seemed fine with that, but when Owen showed up at Sweet Breeze the next morning and found her already out on the sidewalk stretching, her tiny running shorts and tank top revealing a lot of her tan skin, his blood ran hot. And he hadn't even started exercising yet.

"Morning," he said in his most placid voice. He noticed she had new shoes and wondered if she'd run as fast today as she normally did.

"Hey." She grinned at him and came toward him like she'd step right into his arms and hug him.

When she did exactly that, Owen wasn't sure what to do. Breathing seemed normal, and he took a long drag of the scent of her hair—which was totally the wrong thing to do if he wanted to keep their relationship on the down-low.

"Mm," he said. "You smell like coffee and peaches."

Her arms around him tightened and then released, and he let her step away. "You ready?" She lifted her knees, and Owen almost groaned.

"I'm old," he said. "Keep that in mind, please. And we haven't run for two weeks."

She simply grinned, and he liked that he'd gotten his flirty, fun Gina back. Her therapy was obviously helping, and he knew she'd been out with Lexie and Sasha shopping too.

He let her set the pace as they ran east, away from Sweet Breeze, and down the road that curved toward Stacey's bed and breakfast. The rhythm of his feet didn't take long to find, and Gina did run a little slower than she had a couple of weeks ago.

"So I have a truth for you," she said between breaths.

"Already?"

"It's about running."

"Okay, shoot."

"I only started a few years ago, when my partner left. Remember I told you about that?"

Owen remembered, and he was glad she was telling him more important things than what kind of cake was her favorite. Though he'd liked learning about the German chocolate obsession, as well as the fact that she'd never owned a dog, was allergic to artichokes, and wanted to travel the world, it wasn't the deep information he wanted to know about her.

"Yeah," Gina said. "I lost about fifty pounds, actually." She glanced at Owen. "Because of the running."

"Do you actually like running?" he asked.

"I like that it gives me something to focus on," she said. "My therapist in Texas wanted me to find something outside of closets, outside of the business, to care about. I chose running."

Part of Owen wished she'd chosen something a little less

physical—like jigsaw puzzles—but he did enjoy spending time with her first thing in the morning, with only palm trees for witnesses.

They made it to their halfway point and turned around to head back to the hotel. A tiki torch in someone's front yard caught his eye, and he said, "Hey, I forgot to ask you."

"Yeah?"

He timed his breathing, hoping he could talk. Wow, it was amazing how out of shape he'd gotten in only two weeks. "There's a luau next weekend Sweet Breeze is sponsoring. Maybe we could go together?"

She tripped over her own feet and almost went down. Owen's hand shot out and grabbed her arm, steadying her.

"Like, a date?" She slowed her pace until they were almost walking. She was red-faced and sweaty, and Owen almost wanted to stop and walk back.

"Yes," he said. "Like a date. Isn't that what we've been doing? Dating?"

"Hanging out in a closet isn't dating."

"Sure, it is," he said. "It's our brand of dating under the radar."

"So would the luau be over the radar?"

"No," he said. "You live at Sweet Breeze. We can simply sit by each other."

"Will the boys be there?"

"Yes," he said, quickly adding, "But Fisher and Stacey have asked them to sit with them at the head table." He sucked at the air. "So it would just be me and you. Nothing more than what we do at the bagelry or the bistro. Everyone sees us do that." Owen would like to take their relationship out of the shadows, but he sure did like keeping it private too.

"All right," she said. "I've never been to a luau."

"They're pretty fun," he said. "Great food, great entertainment." He couldn't talk anymore, not with his lungs on fire as they were.

"And you're coming to see the system that was delivered yesterday?" she asked.

"Yes," he almost grunted out. "Sometime this afternoon." He managed to make it back to the hotel with her, and she didn't seem nearly as out of shape as he did, which hardly seemed fair as she was the one who'd sustained a head injury.

As they walked down the beachwalk toward the copse of trees that separated the bigger bay where Sweet Breeze sat from the east bay, he thought it would be natural to take her hand in his and lead her down to the water.

Kiss her. Hold her close to his heart, and tell her he'd been thinking so much about her and ask her if she was falling as fast as he was.

But they never held hands during their cool-down.

She started a story about one of her foster families, and Owen kept his fantasies dormant by listening to her, trying to support her, and then pausing when they reached the trees.

Gina finished with, "It wasn't the worst house I'd been in. Huge lawn though, and I had to mow it every week."

He turned toward her and said, "How long were you there?"

"Nine months." She met his eye and stretched up on her

toes, her lips skating against his cheek before he could process a single thought.

"Thank you, Owen." She settled back on her feet, but his name in her voice poured through his mind like warm coffee on a cold day.

"For what?" he managed to ask.

"For letting me figure things out."

"How's that coming?" He went with her as she started back toward the hotel.

"Good." She smiled at the ground and then at him. "Really good."

"Must be," he said with a hint of sarcasm in his voice.

"Why do you say that?"

"Because you just kissed me in front of your Beach Club." He nodded toward the three women sunning themselves a dozen yards down the beach, all of them looking at Owen and Gina.

# ELEVEN

GINA FROZE, her heart bobbing somewhere between her nose and the back of her throat. "Oh, great," she whispered, horror in the two syllables.

"It's fine," he said, nudging her toward them. "Just tell them I fixed a problem for you and it was a show of gratitude." He bent his head toward hers. "Which it was. Not a lie."

A shiver from his breath against her neck made her shudder slightly. Then he retreated, straightening and waving to Stacey, Tawny, and Sasha before saying, "See you later, Gina."

He walked away without a care in the world, leaving her to face her friends alone. Which was fine. She didn't need to try to invent a reason for why she'd just kissed him on the cheek with him standing beside her.

Stacey waved at her to come join them, and Gina stepped onto the sand, excuses running through her mind.

"Hey, guys," she said, taking a spot of sand though the grains stuck to her skin in an uncomfortable way. "You're out early today."

"I have to teach at eight," Tawny said.

"My stand opens at eleven," Sasha added.

"And I just needed some sun early," Stacey said. "You're running again?"

"Yep." Gina popped the P. "Feeling great."

"Obviously." Tawny lowered her shades. "I'm pretty sure I just saw you kiss Owen Church."

"Oh, no." Sasha shook her head emphatically. "Don't you remember she's told us over and over *and over* that they're just friends?" Her tone carried only sarcasm, and she flashed a friendly smile at Gina.

"Yeah, because I kiss all my friends on the cheek too," Stacey said.

"They do in Australia," Gina said. Or she thought they did. "England. All of Europe, actually."

All three women looked at her, and Gina shrugged. "He did something to save me some embarrassment with the closets. I was just saying thank you."

"With your lips." Sasha quirked one eyebrow.

"How else do you thank someone?" Gina asked, throwing some attitude right back at her friend. Besides Lexie, Sasha was Gina's closest friend.

"A note," Stacey said.

"Email," Tawny added. "Text. A gift card. Cup of coffee."

Gina started laughing and said, "All right. I get it."

Her friends grinned at each other like they were about to

get a real treat. Gina closed her eyes and let the morning Hawaii sun bathe her in golden light.

She'd never felt this content in Texas, not even when Classy Closets had been named one of the fastest growing companies in the world, or when her shares had topped one billion dollars.

"So?" Stacey said, shattering Gina's peace. "Are we going to get the real story?"

Gina opened her eyes, a decision made. "Yeah," she said. "I'm moving here permanently. Will you guys help me find a house?"

They clearly weren't expecting that, but Sasha recovered first. "There are nice places up where I live. I could check and see if there are any for sale."

"Sure," Gina said. "Thanks, Sasha."

"I'm not helping until I know if you're dating Owen," Tawny said, her voice a bit on the petulant side.

Owen's words about how he wouldn't hide the relationship from his sons cascaded through Gina's mind. If she told her friends, she would essentially be admitting she was ready to take their undercover relationship into the light.

"I'm not quite sure." She spoke slowly, as if she didn't know how he felt about her. But she saw the way he watched her, the desire in his eyes whenever they were alone together, the deliberate questions to draw her outside of herself.

The door between them was definitely open, but she hadn't invited him in all the way yet.

If she told her friends, she could. And that was as scary as it was appealing.

"Do you like him?" Tawny asked.

"Yes," Gina said honestly. "There's a lot about him to like. Some things I'm still working through." That much was true. She looked at her friends. "So, can I pass with a maybe?"

Stacey grinned and nodded. "Works for me. But I want details as maybe moves into yes."

"What if it doesn't?" Gina asked.

"Oh, please, girl. Have you seen the way that man looks at you? He's just waiting for your maybe to become a yes too." Stacey settled back into her beach chair, her participation in the conversation clearly over.

Gina looked at Sasha, who said, "I agree with Stacey. And Owen's a great guy."

He was a great guy, and when Gina asked, "So, Tawny, will you help me find a place?" the beach yoga instructor said, "Sure. Do you want a big house like Jasper's or something more low-key, like a condo or a beach house?"

Gina had no idea what she wanted. "I'll think about it." Sometimes not having dreams made the simplest of tasks difficult. As a teenager, she simply wanted control. Organizing things had been so appealing to her, she'd seized on that in college and done whatever it took to get her degrees and get her business off the ground.

She'd never much cared where she lived, but as she laid on the beach with her friends, she let her imagination run wherever it wanted.

By the time Tawny started packing up, Gina knew. She got up with Tawny and said goodbye to the other women.

As they walked back to Sweet Breeze together, Gina said,

"I want a house. But nothing huge. Something quaint, with a small yard." Something she could organize and control on her insane schedule.

Tawny grinned and hugged her. "I'll start looking around. I have a friend who's a real estate agent. Oh! Did you know Owen used to sell real estate?"

Gina had not known that, and she said as much. "Maybe I'll ask him."

"I would." Tawny waved as she detoured toward her class beach area, where a few people had already gathered.

Gina went up to her room, showered, and went down to the suites on the fifth floor. She put the shelves on the hardware she'd installed yesterday.

The island had been installed a few days ago, and she pulled open the whisper-quiet drawers and let them slide back closed again.

"This is perfect." The formal wear rack had been hung yesterday, and now she needed to get the full-length mirrors in the dressing room that somehow Owen had worked his magic to get built in only ten days.

Gina worked in the silence, letting her mind focus on the tasks at hand. Everything else faded away, just like it did when she ran, and she made all the lines match up, the corners at perfect ninety-degree angles.

She finished just after noon and stood in the corner, admiring the perfect organization that could happen in here now.

She stepped into the dressing room just as Owen did, almost knocking heads with him.

"Oh." She cried out and stumbled back. Her heart

leapfrogged itself and then settled as she took in his perfect physique and stylist suit.

"I wasn't expecting you until later."

"I passed a job to someone else." He gazed at himself in the mirror. "This looks great."

"There will be a bench here." She indicated the long wall facing the door that entered the closet. "But they won't come until almost the end."

"This is the end," Owen said. "They'll be done in the main part in a couple of days."

Gina spun toward him. "So I should order the benches?"

"Yes, then we can start renting this room."

"Oh, I thought we were doing them all and then renting."

Owen looked at her, his business face in place. "No, we want to rent as the rooms become available."

Gina's nerves didn't like this change of plans. "Is there somewhere for me to store the benches?"

"Of course."

"So I'll get those ordered today. I've got enough systems for all the one-bedroom units."

"And four of them are waiting for you."

Four. Waiting for her to get them under control. She wanted to start working on the next one immediately, despite the pinch in her calves that said she shouldn't have run so fast or so far this morning.

She started nodding and couldn't stop. "I'll move on to the next one today."

"All right." Owen's face softened and he let his fingers

drift down her bare arm. "What did you tell your friends this morning."

Gina leaned into him, the crisp, masculine scent of him so irresistible. "We're at the maybe stage."

"So you didn't lie."

Gina jerked back. "You think we're at the maybe stage?"

Owen's expression darkened. "Well, we haven't…taken the next step. Feels like maybe to me. Which I'm fine with," he rushed to add. "Honestly, I am."

But Gina thought she heard a note of doubt in his voice.

"By the way, I like these shorts with the camo pockets." He grinned down and her. "Do you have time for lunch?"

"What time is it?" He pinged from one subject to another so quickly, Gina couldn't keep up.

"Almost one."

"I have an appointment at two-fifteen."

"So a quick lunch." He threaded his fingers through her ponytail and wrapped his arms around her. "Yes?"

"Yes." She leaned into him, so far that if he let go of her, she'd fall. She had a distinct feeling in that moment that she'd been falling for a while now. Falling in love with the handsome general manager.

"What does it take to get to the next level with you?" she asked, her gaze dropping to his mouth. The need to kiss him reached epic proportions, but she forced herself to wait. She had no idea what she was doing. She hadn't kissed a man in a very, very long time, and she had no idea if she was even any good at it.

"I don't know," he said in a husky voice. "We haven't told Zach and Cooper about us. We haven't kissed. We—"

"So if we kiss, I can get us out of maybe?"

"Maybe," Owen said playfully, his grip tightening along her waist.

Her pulse volleyed around her body, almost painfully. "Owen?"

"Mm?" He swayed slightly, and she looked up to find his eyes already closed.

"I'm going to kiss you now." She stretched up and he leaned down, and the first touch of his lips to hers sent fire roaring through her.

He pulled back slightly, and then claimed her mouth completely, this time not a peck, not a touch or a brush, but a *kiss*.

And wow, the man, despite not dating for a decade, certainly knew how to make her feel treasured as he kissed her and kissed her and kissed her.

# TWELVE

OWEN HAD NOT BEEN KISSED by a woman in a long, long time. He'd forgotten the gentle touch of female fingertips along his neck, his ear, and up into his hair.

He never wanted to stop kissing Gina, as he'd been dreaming of this moment for a while now. So he simply kept kissing her, letting her take the lead on when to stop.

Every sense in his body heightened, and Owen felt like he'd taken that first step on a journey to which there was no return.

Gina finally sighed and pulled back, pressing her forehead to his collarbone. "I haven't kissed anyone for a while," she whispered.

"Well, you're a pro." His own voice sounded like he'd just gargled with sand.

She giggled, tipping her head back to look at him. "If my friends ask about us, I won't be able to deny a kiss."

"I wouldn't want you to." Though the thought of

everyone knowing what had just happened in this dressing room made Owen's stomach fill with angry wasps, he was ready to kiss Gina whenever he wanted.

"And we have to tell Cooper and Zach before your Beach Club friends."

Gina stiffened in his arms, but she relaxed a moment later. "When do we want to do that?"

"As soon as possible." He stepped back and let his arms drop to his sides. He felt a bit empty without her right beside him, in his arms. "Dinner tonight? My place? I'll order pizza."

"I like pizza." She tucked her hands in her back pockets. "And I'll be ready to talk to them, I swear."

"We can do it tomorrow night. You'll just have to hibernate in your room."

"Or get to work on those other suites."

Owen leaned against the doorway. "You tell me, Gina."

Gina's eyes searched his, finally saying, "Tonight, Owen. I don't want to be maybe with you anymore."

Happiness tugged and pulled, then raced through Owen. "Tonight," he repeated before drawing her back in for another kiss.

———

After she left for her appointment with her therapist, Owen texted his kids, telling them it would be pizza night at the house and that he had something he wanted to talk to them about.

Zach confirmed first, followed with a picture of an envelope from UCLA.

Owen's breath lodged somewhere in his chest. *Is that a scholarship packet?* he sent.

*I don't know. We'll open it together tonight.*

Owen wondered if he should tell them he was bringing a woman home—his girlfriend.

*I have news too,* Cooper sent.

*Basketball?* Owen asked, realizing he was asking for all the details now instead of waiting until tonight.

*Yes,* Cooper confirmed as Owen's thumbs flew across the screen. He read the message once, and then twice.

Finally he just sent it. *I'm bringing Gina. We've started dating.*

It was simple. No lies. No hidden messages. Neither Zach nor Cooper responded right away, and his heart hammered in the back of his throat.

*That's great, Dad,* Zach finally said, immediately followed by *Yeah, great,* from Cooper.

Owen couldn't really tell if they thought it was great or not —the curse of a text—but they could talk about it that night.

He sent *8:30* and flipped over his phone so he could get some work done.

He fed the tropical fish in the huge tank set into the wall, worked through several scenarios with the grounds crew manager where they could get in a few more trees for their patio area, and then went to a city meeting about the property over in east bay that a big hotel conglomerate had put an offer on last fall.

The family was going to sell initially, but Owen hoped they wouldn't. They already had the building and the land, and if they got the resort back into shape, it would be better than having an outsider come in. He'd already been through that once with Sweet Breeze, and it had turned out well enough, despite the early community protests.

He ordered the pizza around seven and then went up to Gina's room to pick her up. She opened the door while she unrolled one last curler.

"How do I look?" She shook her head, the curls cascading just to the tops of her shoulders.

"Fantastic." Owen admired her slim figure in a classic pair of dark jeans, which she'd paired with a cream blouse with red flowers all over it.

"Shopping successes?" he asked as he entered her room.

She sat on the coffee table and slipped on a pair of red heels, which brought her closer to his height when she stood and said, "Yep."

"Well, you're gorgeous." He drew her into his arms and kissed her, glad he could do exactly what he thought about doing instead of suppressing the urge to touch her.

"Mm." He broke their connection but kept her tucked next to him. "How was your appointment?"

"Really good." She beamed up at him. "And I'm starving, so I hope you got a lot of pizza."

"Define a lot." Owen caught her hand in his as she plucked her purse from the end table. "And I got double pepperoni for you. None of us will eat that, so you should have a whole pizza to yourself."

"What do you eat if not pepperoni?"

Owen chuckled at the genuine surprise on her face. "Supreme, with extra olives. That's what Cooper likes. Zach likes the chicken parmesan one. It actually has noodles on it." He full-on laughed at the horrified look on Gina's face.

"And I like the chicken garlic ranch—with scallops."

Gina made a fake choking noise. "Seafood does not belong on pizza."

"Seafood belongs on everything," Owen said. "Come on, we'll have to wait to pick it up, and I told the boys eight-thirty."

Gina moved with him, stepping into the hall first without letting go of his hand. "So," she said swinging their hands between them. "What did you tell them about tonight?"

"I told them I was bringing you, and that you were my girlfriend."

Her curls fell between them as she ducked her head. "What did they say?"

"They said 'that's great, Dad.' I don't know what that means. Texting isn't a good medium for important conversations."

"No, not usually." She practically danced onto the elevator, pulling him into another kiss as the doors slid closed behind her. "I've always wanted to kiss someone on an elevator," she said, giggling. Owen obliged, because he wanted to kiss Gina everywhere, anywhere, whenever, however.

She pulled back and stroked her fingers through his hair, her blue eyes bright and serious at the same time. "I really like you, Owen."

"I really like you too, Gina." He gazed back at her, glad she seemed so whole and well since her fall a few weeks ago.

The elevator opened to the lobby, and he stepped away from her. He didn't want to go around flaunting the relationship, especially where he worked, and they did need to wait until the boys were looped in.

At Woodfire, Owen cuddled with Gina on a bench near a faux fireplace while they waited for their order. He told her about the snorkeling on the island, the luau next week, and the yacht club.

"You sail?" she asked.

"I grew up here," he said. "Learning to sail is like learning to walk."

She smiled but the excitement in her eyes wasn't quite as bright as when they'd talked about snorkeling. "The ocean scares me a little," she said.

"But you want to get in it and put your head under?"

"That's different than going out on a boat."

"It is? How? And by the way, there's some very good snorkeling out at the reef. Way better than the cove."

"It just…feeling like I could get lost out in a boat. Like I have no control over if I'll be able to get back."

Owen nodded, noting her use of the word *control*. She'd told him once that having control of things, organizing them and making them line up, was very important to her. He'd known that, as she'd once organized the folders on his desk while they ate lunch in his office.

But this time, something different pricked his heart. If she couldn't control their relationship, would she end it?

Owen didn't let the thought stay long, and Matt called

his name to pick up the pizzas anyway. From there, it was just fifteen minutes to the house, and then the conversation would be all about him and Gina and the new relationship they'd started.

He shouldn't be thinking about it ending already. He frowned as he paid for the pizza, wondering if his negativity toward relationships was why he hadn't dated since his divorce. Did he automatically assume every relationship would break apart, splinter, disintegrate, the way his had?

He remained quiet on the drive to his home around the curve on the island, realizing that yes, he did believe most relationships ended.

But he'd seen others survive. Thrive, even. Stacey and Fisher seemed happy. They didn't have children yet, and Owen knew what a challenge that was for any couple.

His own parents had been split up by the early death of his mother, and as he pulled into his driveway, he realized he had a problem to overcome. If he wanted to become part of Gina's life, he'd have to figure out a way to believe that what they were doing would last.

Gina smoothed down her blouse, a showing of her own nerves, and Owen slid his management mask into place.

"They're going to be fine," he told her. "No surprises tonight." He climbed the steps to the front door and paused. "Well, maybe one. Zach has a big envelope from UCLA. Could be a scholarship. He's going to open it with us tonight."

Gina smiled, ran her fingers through her hair one more time, and nodded Owen into the house.

# THIRTEEN

GINA DIDN'T FEEL QUITE the same calmness inside Owen's house tonight as she had the previous morning. He led the way down the hall to the kitchen, where both of his sons sat at the counter, their phones in front of them.

"Hey, Dad," Cooper said, his eyes flickering over to Gina. "Hi, Gina." He stood and extended his hand for her to shake.

Gina smiled at him and shook his hand. "I hear you're an all-star basketball player."

Cooper grinned from ear to ear and shook his head. "Not quite."

Owen slid the boxes of pizza on the counter and said, "Zach, get down some plates, would you? Cooper, grab the paper towels."

Both boys complied without complaint, and Gina liked how they worked together though the tasks were simple.

"Is this it?" Owen asked, picking up a large white envelope.

Zach said, "Yes." He put the plates next to the boxes. "Should we do news first?" He glanced at Gina too, a smile barely touching his mouth before it disappeared.

"I want to know what's in this." Owen shook the envelope and turned to Cooper. "And what news you have about basketball." He stepped back over to Gina and laced his fingers through hers, clearing his throat roughly. "And obviously, we might need to talk about me and Gina."

The silence that followed felt strained to Gina despite her best attempts to smile and charm the boys without saying anything.

"So I'll go," Cooper said. "Coach made me a permanent starter on the varsity team." He beamed at Owen and Zach, who both beamed back.

"That's great." Owen hugged his son and clapped him on the back. "Great job, Cooper. You've worked hard for that." He put his arm around his son's shoulders and faced Gina. "He gets up early every morning to work out, do drills, all of it." He grinned down at Cooper. "I'm glad your hard work is paying off."

"Thanks, Dad."

"Good job, Coop." Zach high-fived his brother and picked up the envelope. "I guess I'm next."

And then Gina would have to endure a conversation about her, while she stood there and listened. Her stomach rumbled for want of food, but she wasn't sure she'd be able to eat more than a few bites at most.

"Open it," Owen said, quickly moving into a chant with Cooper. "Open it, open it, open it!"

Zach shook his head as he smiled, though he obviously enjoyed the attention. He ripped open the flap of the envelope and pulled out a few sheets of paper. After clearing his throat, he said, "Dear Zachary Church. Congratulations! You have been accepted into the University of California, Los Angeles."

He looked up, his eyes bright. "I got in, Dad."

"Of course you got in." Owen spoke without a trace of doubt. "This one studies and studies. Great grades. High test scores." The pride in his son was obvious, and Gina wondered what it would feel like to have a parent care about her the way Owen obviously cared about his sons.

She had no idea. No one had ever cared what kind of grades or test scores she got. Except for her. No one told her good job. No one brought home pizza and had a celebratory night with good news.

She felt like an imposter. One hundred percent like she didn't belong with Owen or his family. She stayed rooted to the spot, though, not wanting to ruin this night for him.

"It says what day they start...." Zach's eyes scanned the first page and he slid it behind the others.

His gaze zipped from side to side as he read silently, then a smile burst onto his face. "We're pleased to offer you the UCLA Regents Scholarship, based on your academic merit. This is a one-year scholarship in the amount of twenty-four thousand dollars, which can be renewed on a yearly basis."

He looked up from the papers, his face holding a range of emotions.

"The Regents Scholarship!" Owen practically yelled. "Zach, that's huge."

Zach shook his head, the smile fading from his face. "Dad, the out-of-state tuition is way more than this scholarship." He looked down at the pages again, scanning them. "This is enough for resident tuition." He slid them back in the envelope. "I'll wait and see what the university here offers."

"Zach." Owen gently took the envelope from his son and pulled out the papers to look at them himself. "If this is what you want, I can afford to send you to California for college."

"I'll give you a scholarship," Gina said, unsure of where the words had come from.

Zach looked at her with wariness and Owen with surprise.

"I mean, I have money."

Owen smiled at her, the kind of smile she'd give to a small child. "I have money too, Gina."

"You do?" They'd never really talked about their finances, and why should they? He knew she went to Fisher's fancy billionaire meetings. And he worked for the richest man on the island. Surely the salary was nothing to sneeze at.

"I don't know, Dad," Zach said, interrupting their conversation. "I'll think about it."

"We can afford it," Owen repeated, scanning the pages. "Maybe this would pay for your books and housing. It's a great scholarship, Zach."

"You don't even want me to go to UCLA."

"No," Owen said slowly. "I don't." He picked up a plate

and opened one of the pizza boxes. "Because I don't want you that far away. I want to be able to see you more often." He pushed the box off the stack and tried the next one. "But Zach, this isn't about me. I know that. You do what you feel is right." He slid a slice of pizza covered with all kinds of heinous things onto his plate. "And I'll support you."

He indicated the plates. "Come on, guys, let's eat. Gina." He set his plate down and moved boxes around until he found the pizza with the double pepperoni in it. Owen put two slices on a plate and handed it to her. "We'll eat at the table tonight."

Gina took the food and went to the dining table in front of a set of French doors that opened into a back yard. A moment later, Owen sat beside her. Within a few seconds, everyone had their food and was seated at the table.

No one spoke, and she thought maybe that was it. Owen had brought her home, and neither of his kids had been surprised. He ate through one slice of pizza and then wiped his mouth.

"So, boys, Gina and I have just started dating. We wanted to tell you first, so you wouldn't hear about it from Fisher or Stacey or someone else." He looked at both boys and then Gina. "It's still pretty new, and we're going pretty slow, and honestly, I'm surprised she hasn't broken up with me yet." He grinned at her. "How do you guys feel about that?"

Cooper kept his eyes on his pizza, but Zach looked back and forth between Gina and Owen. "She's younger than you, Dad."

"True. Not too much younger though."

"Ten years," Gina said. "It's kind of a significant number of years."

"Does it bother you?" Owen asked, and Gina marveled at how he asked hard questions and entertained sensitive topics right in front of his kids.

"No," Gina said.

"Doesn't bother me either," Owen said. "She's closer to my age than yours, Zach. So it's probably okay."

"Okay."

Still, it felt like Zach was sizing her up. "Were you dating her when she stayed here a couple of weeks ago?"

"No," Owen said.

"So it's really new."

"Really new," Owen confirmed. "Like, when?" He looked at Gina. "Maybe right after that?"

"Our first date was lunch the next day," she said. "I think. I had a head injury, so I'm sort of fuzzy on the details."

Owen chuckled and took her hand in his. "We've been friends for a few months, and she works at Sweet Breeze. So we know a bit about each other, and we're just seeing how things go."

*Just seeing how things go.* Gina really liked the sound of that. It was non-threatening. Casual. Easy.

"What else?" Owen asked.

"Have you been married before?" Cooper asked.

"No," Gina said.

"So no kids."

She swallowed and squeezed Owen's hand. "No kids." Thankfully, her voice only sounded slightly strangled.

"Have you kissed?" Zach asked.

Gina sucked in a breath, but Owen said, "Just today, actually."

Zach nodded and went back to his food, his curiosity apparently satisfied. Cooper didn't say anything else, and Owen continued to eat like discussing his private love life with two teenagers was perfectly normal.

Gina appreciated the open and honest communication, she really did. It just felt so...odd. She'd never had anyone to talk with like this, and she didn't know the first thing about doing it. She was so far out of her element that she couldn't eat or contribute to the conversation that sprang up about graduation announcements, then the upcoming sweethearts dance at school, or the basketball game schedule.

It felt like a long time before they started clearing their dishes and the boys disappeared into their bedrooms, leaving her and Owen alone.

He led her to the couch, where he sat and tucked her into his side. "So." He dipped his mouth to her ear and kissed her there. "What did you think? Terrible?"

"No," she said, leaning into his touch. "It was just... different than anything I've done before."

"I bet." He trailed his lips along her throat. "I thought it went really well. Only a few questions, and I didn't feel any resistance from either one of them."

She was glad he hadn't. She hadn't been able to read them at all, Zach especially. She lowered her chin and met Owen's mouth with hers. This kiss felt different than the others they'd shared. It was slower, touched with more passion, and struck her deeper emotionally.

"I like them," she whispered.

"I'm glad." Owen held her close. "I think they like you too."

"Is Zach really going to go to California for college?"

"Seems like he wants to." Owen sighed. "And you know I have quite a bit of money, right? I used to sell real estate back in the heyday of the housing market. I've got more than enough to help Zach pay his out-of-state tuition."

Foolishness raced through her. "I blurt things out sometimes. It's a flaw."

"A cute one." He chuckled and touched his lips to her forehead.

"I wanted to talk to you about something too," she said.

"Oh?" Owen eased back so he could look at her.

"Yeah." Gina pushed his hair off his forehead. "I'm looking for a place to buy, and seeing how you used to be in real estate, I'm wondering if you can refer me to someone who can help with that."

His eyebrows shot toward his hairline. "You're looking to buy? Here in Getaway Bay?"

"Well, I'm going to be working here for several months, and I sort of have this handsome boyfriend now, and maybe I won't go back to Dallas." She shrugged like such a major life change was no big deal.

"Boyfriend," he repeated as if he'd never thought of himself as such a thing before.

"Not just any boyfriend," Gina said, leaning into him again. "The *billionaire's* boyfriend."

He laughed and she joined in with him, happier and more content than she thought she could ever be.

Gina allowed herself to enjoy the moment, as Doctor White had counseled her to do. "You have to allow yourself to be happy," she'd said that afternoon. "The only one stopping you from feeling that joy of being in a relationship with a man, is you, Gina."

And she'd been right. So maybe Owen had one leg through the doorway now. The thought of inviting him all the way into her life still scared Gina to death, and she coached herself to take one little step at a time.

Reveal one more truth. Keep him for one more day. She only hoped she wouldn't end up with a broken heart by the end of everything.

# FOURTEEN

MAYBE I WON'T GO BACK *to Dallas.*

Gina's words looped through Owen's mind for a week. But she didn't seem to be looking for a place—at least she hadn't asked him to help her.

His real estate license was still good; he made sure it didn't expire. No reason to make life difficult down the road if he wanted to go back to the profession.

The night of the luau arrived, and he changed out of his sky blue dress shirt and into a more tropical button-down that sent a quiver of embarrassment through him.

"You look ridiculous," he muttered to himself as he combed his hair to the side. But he couldn't go to a luau in a business suit. He'd tried that before, and the mocking was more than he'd get in this bright, colorful shirt, which had a bird on it.

A *bird.*

He turned away from his reflection in disgust just as

Gina opened the door and said, "Knock, knock." She looked toward his desk first and then swung her attention toward him.

"Oh. My." She pressed one palm to her heart.

"Go ahead and laugh."

Gina's face burst into a smile, and the laugher wasn't far behind. "It's not bad," she said, advancing toward him. "Honest. It's just so not you."

"I'm aware." He couldn't help smiling at her though. "You look nice."

She wore a black dress with thin straps over her shoulders and a hemline that fell to her knees. The big, bold flowers all over it screamed luau, and a pair of peacock feathers dangled from her ears.

"This totally fits you." He pushed a lock of her hair behind her ear and leaned down to kiss her.

All of his questions piled up in his mind, but he hadn't let himself say them this week. Things had gone so well at dinner last week, and their time spent together this week had been magical. He didn't need to ruin things with his curiosity.

"I saw Fisher and Stacey on their way out with the boys," Gina whispered against his lips. "Should we go?"

"Mm, yes." Owen kept kissing her though, not quite ready to downgrade to hand-holding.

She let him carry on for several more seconds and then giggled as she pulled back. "Come on, Romeo. We're going to be late."

"You obviously haven't been to a luau."

Gina jerked and looked over her shoulder at him.

"I mean—"

"No," she said, something hard covering her features for a moment. "I haven't been to a luau."

Owen's hand automatically went to his throat to adjust his tie, but he wasn't wearing one. Even his nervous tics would have to be adjusted for tonight.

"Well, the first half-hour is entertainment," he said. "While everyone gets seated. We won't be late."

"I like to be entertained." Gina threw him a flirty smile and left his office, her pink-sandaled feet slapping against the tile.

He couldn't keep up with her moods, but he had longer strides than her and caught up to her easily in the hall, capturing her hand in his before they made it to the registration desk.

"I didn't mean anything by it," he said, glancing around like he expected a riot to break out at any moment.

"I know."

They arrived at the luau a few minutes later, where a Hawaiian woman wearing traditional clothing put a lei around each of their necks. They received table assignments, put in drink requests, and allowed the usher to lead them to their seats.

Music filtered down from the speakers in the tent above, and fans and misters kept the air cool. Owen wanted to take his shoes off so they wouldn't be full of sand, but he didn't.

Gina dug her toes in and glanced around with an air of excitement. "This is beautiful."

Flowers in every color and size adorned the poles holding up the tents, as well as took center stage on the tables. Flashy prints, palm leaves, and tiki torches completed the festive atmosphere.

An "ah" went up from the crowd to his left, and Owen nudged Gina so she'd watch them bring out the kālua pig.

"Oh, holy cow." Gina looked at him with wide eyes, like it was her first time allowed in a giant candy store and she'd just been told she could have whatever she wanted.

"No, sweetheart," Owen whispered, putting his arm around Gina and bringing her dangerously close to him. "It's a pig."

She laughed and settled back into his chest, right where he wanted to keep her forever.

It took four men to carry the pig to its place in the center of the tent. Women followed, dressed in traditional garments, carrying platters of potatoes, vegetables, fish, poi, and taro leaves. With the introduction of the food, Owen's mouth started to water.

He couldn't remember if he'd eaten lunch or not, and his own enthusiasm for the event grew.

Dancers came out, the music got turned up, and the party really started. Owen clapped along with everyone else, cheered, and lost himself to a tradition he hadn't enjoyed in entirely too long.

He reveled in Gina's reactions, and once again, he didn't want to ruin their experience with his questions. So he saved them for later, when they could be alone, instead of at a table with guests from the hotel.

Afterward, Gina linked her arm through his and said, "That was the best thing I've ever been to."

Owen chuckled and pressed a kiss to her temple. "I'm glad you liked it."

"Do you want to walk with me?" She indicated the beachwalk to the west instead of following the other patrons into Sweet Breeze on the east.

"Sure." He stepped onto the boards, glad to be out of the annoying sand. "I want to take my shoes off."

"Do it." Gina's eyes held a challenge in them.

"You don't think I will." Owen cocked one eyebrow at her.

"No, sir, I don't think you will."

Owen immediately sat on the edge of the beachwalk and started untying his shoes.

Gina laughed beside him. "I can't believe it. I've never seen you with anything unbuttoned, unlaced, or unstrung."

Owen finished taking off his shoes, her words playful but stinging him. He stood, his shoes dangling from a couple of fingers on his right hand. He took Gina's in his left.

"What does that mean?"

"It means you're perfect."

Owen laughed, their steps slower in the sand. But without his shoes on, he didn't mind. "I'm far from perfect, Gina."

"Name one thing."

"I work too much."

"So do I."

It was true. She did work too much. Owen hadn't minded—or even noticed—until he wanted to spend time with her in the evenings.

"I have bad handwriting."

"True."

"I eat my food all mixed together."

"It could be overlooked as a lovable quirk."

"I'm too refined."

"No one would say that if they saw you wearing that shirt."

Owen's next flaw came to mind, but he didn't want to say it out loud.

"Go on," Gina said, the teasing quality of her voice light and fun. "I know you have something else."

"I ask too many questions."

"Ah." She nodded, her gaze settling somewhere on the horizon in front of them. "Now that's a true flaw. Nosy. Wants to know everything, all the time, about everyone."

His ability to chat with people, get to know them and remember tiny details about them, had earned him the top selling real estate agent for four straight years.

So was it a flaw?

Only for someone who didn't want to answer questions —and Gina definitely did not.

Owen let her comments slide, and their conversation turned to Zach's upcoming graduation and college career.

"Has he heard anything from the University of Hawaii?"

"Nothing yet." Owen realized how dark it was and turned them back to the hotel. "Sunday brunch tomorrow?" he asked once they'd arrived back at Sweet Breeze. "At my place. I'll come over in the afternoon to get some things ready for the week."

"Sure." Gina tipped up on her toes and kissed him, right there in the lobby, while she waited for the elevator to arrive.

Owen cursed the speed of the fancy lifts in this hotel, because the doors opened with a beep much too soon.

Gina kept hold of his collar as she backed up, finally letting her hand drop right before he'd have to start walking. She wore a dreamy smile on her face and said, "'Night, Owen," before stepping into the elevator and letting the doors close between them.

"Night," Owen said to himself—and the dozens of other people buzzing about the lobby—and wondered when he'd fallen all the way in love with Gina Jackson.

———

As the weather warmed, more tourists arrived on the island, which meant more work for Owen. More employees that needed hiring. More disturbances, longer lines at check-in, and if the WiFi went down? It was like the apocalypse had hit Sweet Breeze what with the way people went from pleasant to irate in less time than it took to breathe.

He continued to visit Gina every afternoon, between the madness of check-out and the insanity of check-in, but sometimes he just sat there and watched her work.

She was cute with her tape measure, pencil, and notebook in a feminine tool belt slung around her waist. She also wore a hammer with a bright purple grip, a screwdriver, and various hardware in the little pockets.

She said little about her therapy sessions, and Owen's curiosity felt like it would kill him. He'd mastered leaving his sons alone about what they talked about with the psychologist. After all, his wife's abandonment affected him differently than Gina's past would have.

But she didn't tell him much, if anything, about it. The facts she'd agreed to share about herself each day had dwindled and then stopped altogether.

Owen had learned a lot just by watching, his usual method of discovering the personality quirks of a person. They ran together a few times each week. They shared brunches and lunches and late dinners.

But Owen felt like he'd been stuck in a relationship rut for the past two months.

With only seven weeks until Zach's graduation now, he wouldn't have time to help Gina find a house even if she asked.

Which she hadn't.

She didn't seem to be the only one who couldn't make a decision about what she wanted. Zach's acceptance and full ride scholarship to the University of Hawaii had come weeks ago, and still his son hadn't decided where to go or what to do.

The acceptance deadlines were coming up very soon, and Owen had asked Zach about it so many times, the last question had quickly escalated into an argument.

So Owen had stopped asking. It seemed like he might burst from all the questions he had, but he never did.

Instead, he let everyone give him the silent treatment, asking about getting more milk or how the double vanity in the two-bedroom apartment-suites looked.

Owen didn't care about milk or vanities. He didn't want

to be the dad who let things slide, or the perpetual billionaire's boyfriend.

So he picked up the phone and he called his son. "Look, I just need to talk for a minute," he said. "I know you don't want to hear it, but it's important. You need to make a decision by tonight, or some of your opportunities will be gone."

Silence came through the line. "Just talk to me about it," Owen said, the hint of pleading in his voice. "I can maybe help you think through some things."

Nothing was said, and Owen checked to make sure the call was still connected. It was.

"Zach—"

"I want to go to UCLA, Dad, but I'm not sure if I'm doing it for the right reason."

Owen heard the distress in his son's voice. "Okay, tell me the reason."

Zach once again took ages to respond, and Owen employed every ounce of patience he had.

"Maizee," Zach said. "She's going, and we've been dating for almost a year now."

Surprise and panic and horror mixed inside Owen like three separate winds to make a cyclone. "You have a girlfriend?"

"I've taken her to all the dances, Dad."

"But you never said anything."

"I didn't think I needed to."

Owen watched the tropical fish swim around inside the tank several feet away. "And she's going to UCLA, and you're worried you're just following her there."

"Something like that."

"No," Owen said. "Tell me *exactly* what it is."

"It's that," Zach mumbled. "It's pathetic. And expensive. I should just stay and go to the U of H."

Owen knew emotions—and hormones—were powerful things. "What's the worst that could happen? You go to UCLA and you two break up? Then you just come home the next year. Or you stay and find another girl. There are lots of girls, Zach."

"I know that, Dad."

"I don't care about the money." He did care if his eighteen-year-old son was making adult decisions that would affect him for the rest of his life.

"I feel bad, though," Zach said.

"Do we need to draw out of a hat?"

"I don't know."

"I'll get Chinese tonight, and we'll pick. Okay?"

"Yeah, okay." His son sounded miserable, and Owen hated that.

"Look, I need to say one more thing. Do we need to talk about…responsibility when it comes to girlfriends?"

"Oh, no, Dad. Please."

"You're being smart?"

"Dad."

"What? You think I want to be a grandfather at forty-seven?"

"You'd be forty-eight by the time the baby came," Zach said. "And this is not a conversation we're having. I'm not stupid, and I'm not having sex with her." Zach said it emphatically enough that Owen believed him.

He couldn't be more relieved. "All right then. Chinese tonight. I'll get Cooper to make us the choices."

They hung up and Owen stared at his phone. Eleven minutes. An *eleven minute conversation* had revealed so much about his son—some hard things. Worrisome things—but it had been good.

"You've got to do it." But he didn't want to call Gina and have a difficult, eleven minute conversation.

He dialed her anyway.

# FIFTEEN

GINA SILENCED OWEN'S CALL, rationalizing that she'd be late for her appointment if she took it.

*It could be something quick,* she thought, but she shoved her phone in the side pocket of her purse and reached for the door handle to the building where her therapist worked.

She checked in—four minutes early—and sat down to wait. Deciding to text Owen, she pulled out her phone and typed, *Sorry, almost time for my appointment. Call you after?*

*Sure,* he responded with almost immediately. *I just wanted to talk about us.*

Fear struck Gina right behind the eyes. She knew what Owen wanted. He wanted her to stay on the island. Show some commitment to him and them and everything.

He wanted her to talk about her feelings. Wanted her to open up to him. Wanted her to be a sounding board for him, while he supported her.

The door between them was still open, and though she kissed him, went out with him, held his hand, spent time with him and his kids, she had not invited him into her life yet.

"Gina," the receptionist called, and Gina stuffed her emotions away, the same way she did her device.

"Go on back. She's waiting for you."

"Thank you, Marlin." Gina walked down the hall, her head suddenly pounding the way it had after she'd fallen. She opened the door like she wasn't sure who or what would be on the other side though she'd been here dozens of times.

"Good afternoon, Gina." Doctor White set her phone down and pushed to a standing position from where she leaned against her desk. She wore a warm smile, her dark curls at chin-length, and that trademark sparkle in her eye.

Even when she asked Gina the really tough questions, she seemed happy about it.

"Hey, Doctor White." They embraced and Gina sat in her favorite chair, a yellow armchair that had a foot rest in it if she leaned back far enough.

She set her purse on the floor and reached into it to silence her phone. When she looked at Doctor White again, the woman had a mint extended to her.

Gina took it and unwrapped it while Doctor White settled back against the desk like it was a chair.

"Tell me about something," she said.

"I'm halfway done with the one-bedroom apartment suites," she said. "The hotel has been renting them for their long-term guests, and the feedback has all been positive."

"That's great." Doctor White had a way of speaking so that everything sounded the same. She could've said, "How terrible," in the exact same tone. It had unnerved Gina at first, but now she was used to it. Now, she knew *she* was there to talk, not Doctor White.

"Go on."

"The double vanities are *beautiful*."

"Two work things."

Gina sucked in a big breath. "I don't want to talk about Owen."

"All right." But Doctor White didn't say anything else. Didn't prompt Gina with a different topic. And the only thing swirling through her mind was *Owen, Owen, Owen*.

"I need to start looking for a house."

"You've said that."

And Gina had, for at least six weeks. She'd mentioned it to Owen once, but neither of them had brought it up again.

"I work too much."

"Three work things."

Gina sighed, suddenly not in the mood for therapy today. She'd told Doctor White a lot already, and the woman had coached her through several of her past traumas. She had coping mechanisms in place now, ways to refocus her thoughts when they went down a dangerous path, and she'd let go of so much past baggage.

It was the present stuff that was plaguing her.

"Work is out," Doctor White said. "Have you told Owen any of the things we talked about last time?"

Gina stared straight ahead. "No."

"Tell me the reasons for that."

Gina opened her mouth and let the first thing that came to her mind cross her vocal chords. "Because I'm comfortable with things how they are."

"Ah."

Gina could hear Doctor White's words without her even saying them. *Comfortable doesn't encourage change.*

"Do you think Owen is comfortable?"

Gina pressed her lips together and shook her head. "He just called me. Said he wanted to talk tonight."

"Talking is good."

"Except when it's bad."

"Fatalistic," Doctor Owen said. "Switch that."

"I'm trying."

Doctor White came over to the grouping of chairs and sofas in her office. She always sat on the brown leather couch, far right, kitty corner from Gina. Today was no different.

"I'm not sure why you're here," she finally said. "I want you to come as often as you want. But you haven't done any of the things we discussed last week, and frankly, until you do, I can't take you to the next step."

Gina met her therapist's eyes. "I'm scared."

"I know that." Doctor White leaned forward, those sparkling eyes so earnest. "But fear only holds you back. You need to talk to Owen. You need to address the issues with him. And only then can you decide what to do next. How can you expect to make a decision when you don't have all the facts? Would you do that with your closets?"

"No."

"He's more important than your closets."

Gina knew he was, but she hadn't been treating him that way. "He asks so many questions, and I feel like if I can't give the right answers, he'll break up with me."

"At least then you'll know. Living in this in-between state...you don't like that, remember?"

"I remember." They'd spent three sessions on Gina's control issues, and no, she didn't like living a life where she didn't know what would happen next. Which was exactly why she hadn't advanced anything with Owen. Because she didn't know what would happen next. Would he propose? Did he want more kids? Where would they live? Should she even buy a place if they were going to live in his house?

Her own questions were endless and had plagued her for weeks. So she ran and she organized and she avoided hard topics with Owen like they were a deadly disease.

"I'll tell him tonight."

Doctor White didn't smile. Didn't raise her eyebrows like *I'll believe it when I see it.* She just nodded and clapped her hands against her knees. "Anything else you want to tell me?"

"Nancy," Gina said. "I remembered the name of the woman who used to make me pluck the chickens." Before she'd started with Doctor White, Gina would've shuddered. But her past didn't define her future. Not anymore.

"Ah, yes. Nancy," Doctor White said as if she'd known all along. "Is that chapter closed?"

"I'm going to try eating chicken again," she said. "So I'll let you know." Gina picked up her purse, and Doctor White stood.

"I'm sorry," Gina blurted.

"Nope." Doctor White shook her head. "We don't say that here."

Gina smiled, but it felt a little wobbly. She'd had much harder sessions, but somehow, this one felt so emotional. "I know. Don't apologize for who you are. Just go be someone better."

Doctor White opened the door. "Come back soon, Gina." She said it after every session, and Gina wondered if the woman had anything in her life that haunted her. Hurt her. Hampered her happiness.

She hoped so, and immediately felt bad. But it didn't seem fair if Doctor White wasn't human like the rest of them.

Once in the safety of the shade around the side of the building, Gina reached for her phone at the same time it buzzed.

Panic blipped through her. She wanted to go to Owen on her own terms. Needed a bit more time to get ready to focus her thoughts and address her fears

The screen read *Classy Closets Inc.* and she hurried to answer it, trying to mentally calculate the time difference at the same time. "Hello?"

"Miss Gina?"

"Who is this?" It wasn't Toni, whom she'd been expecting.

"It's Sammy MacGuire, ma'am." Her high-pitched voice seemed made of nerves. "I'm just wondering if you've heard from Toni. She hasn't been in for a few days, and none of us can get ahold of her."

The bottom of Gina's world fell out from underneath her feet. "What?"

"Toni Gavinshaw?" the woman said. "I'm just the receptionist, and people keep callin' for things I don't know nothin' about." She sounded near tears, and Gina was getting close to that too.

"When's the last time you saw Toni?"

"Monday, ma'am."

It was Friday, and Gina knew the volume of business and calls Classy Closets received on a daily basis.

"So you haven't heard from her?"

"No," Gina said. "I'll see what I can find out. Thank you, Sammy, for calling." She hung up before the waver in her voice threatened to swallow her whole.

She employed one of the tactics Doctor White had taught her and switched her thoughts to something more positive.

Her favorite thing on the island: running with Owen. She envisioned the pounding rhythm of their feet, the evenness in her breathing, the steady, comforting presence of him beside her.

When she opened her eyes, she didn't feel like the ground was too brittle to hold her weight.

But she also knew she couldn't wait to get back to Dallas and figure out what was going on. If Toni hadn't been in to work for four days....

Gina refused to let her thoughts spiral. Toni was not Ian. "She's not," she said as she pulled up the number for Esther's car service.

"Hi," she said. "I need a ride to the airport."

While she waited, she called Owen, nowhere near the conversation she wanted to have right now. "Hey there, beautiful," he said by way of greeting.

"Hey," she practically barked. "I know you wanted to talk, but can I get a rain check on it? Something's happened in Dallas, and I need to get back there tonight."

"What happened?" His flirty tone was all business now.

"I don't know," she said as a shiny, black car rounded the corner. She lifted her hand to flag down the driver. "But my general manager is missing." She slid into the car and said, "Airport, please." She had enough money to buy whatever she needed between now and the time she arrived at her house in Texas.

"I'll come with you," Owen said.

"Don't' be silly," she said, softening her words with a giggle. "There's no way Sweet Breeze could function without you."

"Oh, they'd be fine."

"Owen." Gina didn't know what else to say, and hoped that everything she felt for him could be said in four letters and two syllables.

"Fly safe," he said, his voice reverent. "Call me when you land. No matter what time it is."

Gina nodded, feeling foolish that her emotions had chosen now to strike, when he couldn't see her to know she was agreeing with him.

"Okay," she finally managed to push out and she hung up before she could break down completely in front of him.

"No," she said. "Not breaking down over this." And she wouldn't. She'd fly to Texas, find out what was going on, and fix it.

But as she hurried into the airport and joined the line at

the ticket counter, she couldn't help feeling like she'd already done that once. And she wasn't sure she had the strength to do it all over again.

# SIXTEEN

OWEN DID NOT like the idea of Gina flying to Texas overnight. He also had no idea what to do about it. She was a grown woman, with a lot of money. She certainly didn't need him.

His chest tightened as if someone had wrapped a rubber band around it and was twisting.

He pulled into the driveway, his mood as dark as the clouds that had rolled in a few hours ago. The scent of orange chicken and crispy wontons made him want to punch something, but he calmly collected the food and went inside.

Cooper sat on the couch with a book open across his lap, tapping on his phone to check something. "Hey, Dad."

"Hey." Owen practically threw the food on the counter. "Where's Zach?"

"In his room."

Owen went down the hall to the first door on the right,

which was closed. He pounded on it, maybe a little harder than necessary.

*Calm down*, he told himself. He'd endured difficult situations before. Heck, walking in on his wife had been downright humiliating and heart-wrenching. He'd spent a long time in the anger camp too and learned how to get past those debilitating emotions.

But he really needed to talk to Gina, and with their relationship basically paused, he felt completely out of control.

"Zach." He knocked again, this time opening the door a moment later—and came face-to-face with a blonde girl.

Lightning struck him, making him freeze and stare straight at her.

"Dad," Zach said, rushing forward. "Uh, you're home... this is Maizee."

"She's in your room." Owen switched his gaze to Zach. "With the door closed."

"We were just studying."

"Calculus," Maizee said, her voice very much like a squeaky mouse.

Owen had no idea what to do. There was no manual to consult. No pause button he could push until he gained control of his emotions and then consulted the manual that didn't exist.

"It's time for dinner." Owen turned and walked back into the kitchen, footsteps behind him moving toward the front door instead of following him. He methodically got out the white containers of food, pulled plates from the cupboard, and got out forks. "Dinner, Coop."

Cooper set aside his work and came over to the counter.

"How often does Zach bring Maizee home?"

"I don't know." Cooper shrugged and reached for the ham fried rice. "A lot, I guess."

Snakes writhed in Owen's stomach, squirming their way into his bloodstream. Zach walked into the kitchen, guilt practically exuding from his body.

"I'm sorry, Dad."

"Yeah?" Owen almost ripped the flaps on one of the containers. "About what?" He held the Mongolian beef in his hand and stared at his son.

Zach ducked his head and shrugged. "I should've told you about Maizee last fall."

"Yep."

"And not taken her into my room alone."

"Right again."

Zach looked at Owen, all of his emotions streaming across his face. "I haven't done anything stupid."

"You're on strike three," Owen said. "So you'll give me every answer I want until I'm sure you're the smart son I raised." He forked some food onto his plate and took the container from Cooper.

"No girls in boy's bedrooms," he said, the rules for his sons slipping off his tongue as easily as blinking. They knew them. Owen had drilled them into them for months the year Zach had turned fourteen. After all, Owen had been fourteen once too, and it wasn't easy.

"We call or text when we're not going to be home on time. We trust each other with everything." He stabbed his fork at Zach. "I told you about my girlfriend. Kissing and everything." He shook his head, this day about the worst one he'd had since having to call the cops on a woman who'd locked herself in a guest room with her four-year-old son.

"I'm sorry, Dad," Zach said, and he sounded like he was. But sometimes sorry couldn't undo stupid.

"What else do I need to know?" he asked. "I can see your grades online. I get emails and phone calls when you miss even a single period. So at least you're going to class."

"I am," Zach said. "The AP tests are next week. We really were studying."

"And you couldn't do that at the table out here?"

Zach looked at Cooper, and Owen saw it all. "Of course you can. But it's more fun if you can hold her hand or kiss her in between problems, right?"

"Something like that," Zach mumbled.

"*Exactly* like that," Owen said sharply. "And it's not okay. You're not married, and it's not smart to play like you are."

"Like you and Gina?" Zach asked, his eyes blazing now. "I know you sneak off to see her in those closets she's designing."

"I'm an adult," Owen said. "I can make adult decisions and deal with the consequences. You're eighteen-years-old with a world of possibilities in front of you. You want to be an adult and do adult things? Then you have to be willing to pay for those things."

"You said you didn't care about the money."

"For college," Owen said, taking his plate around the counter to the bar. Cooper sat at the end, listening but saying nothing. "But I'm not paying to raise your son."

"Dad, I already said I'm not having sex with her!"

"Who knows what was happening behind that closed door?" Owen hated that he'd raised his voice. He drew in a deep breath through his nose.

"*I* know what's happening behind that closed door," Zach said, practically dumping the entire container of orange chicken on his plate.

Owen felt utterly defeated, and he gave Zach a tired look. "Okay, son. I believe you." The tension remained but at least Zach came around and sat beside Owen. The three of them ate in silence, but Owen was so glad his kids were there, on either side of him. He couldn't imagine his life without them, and he finished his food and said, "I love you guys. I just want you to be happy. Be ready to be an adult, be mature enough to make good choices, and be happy."

"We know, Dad," Cooper said. Owen looked at Zach, who nodded, his jaw tight.

"So." Owen exhaled. "I think we're drawing out of a hat tonight." He looked back and forth between Cooper and Zach. "Right?"

Cooper held up the two slips of paper he'd decorated, and Owen took them from him. But when he faced Zach, he found the boy shaking his head.

"No, Dad, I decided."

"You did?" Owen's heart skipped a couple of beats. "And?"

"And I'm staying here." He got up and retrieved the papers from where they'd been stuck to the fridge for what felt like forever. "I'm going to accept the scholarship and get housing figured out."

He sat beside Owen again, and a swell of pride rose

through Owen, so different from the emotions he'd felt only twenty minutes ago.

"What about Maizee?"

"We're not that serious, Dad."

"You've been dating her for eight months."

"It's a loose term." Zach shrugged.

"Do you kiss her?" Owen really didn't understand how dating could be loose.

"Yeah, sure."

"Would you be mad if she kissed someone else?"

"Of course."

"Sounds like dating to me." Owen looked at Cooper. "What am I missing?"

"He's just not feeling her, right, Zach?"

"I like her, sure," Zach said. "But am I real serious about her? After talking with you this afternoon, Dad, I realized I wasn't." He put the paper down. "I thought about how I'd feel if we went to UCLA and she broke up with me to date someone else. And I didn't care all that much." He shrugged again. "But I like her. I'm not using her or anything. We'll stay friends when she goes off to California." He tapped and typed and swiped on his phone. A few minutes later he said, "Done," and met Owen's eyes.

"I'm proud of you," Owen said. "But I still don't want any girls in your room with the door closed."

"No girls in boy's rooms," Zach said with a smile and Owen pulled him into a hug.

———

Owen woke the next morning, his first thought that he hadn't heard from Gina overnight. He'd expected her to call by now, like she'd said she would.

"Surely she's there." Owen didn't have the flight schedules memorized, but he knew Texas was five hours ahead of them, which meant it was almost eleven o'clock there.

He dialed her number, his heartbeat increasing with every ring. She finally said, "Owen, I have about two minutes."

"Did you make it to Texas?"

"Yes, I'm here."

He didn't know what else to say. *You said you'd call* sounded juvenile and accusatory.

"Okay," he said. "I just wanted to check and make sure."

"Okay," she said.

"So call me when you have more than two minutes."

"Will do." The call ended, and Owen wasn't sure, but he didn't think he'd ever had a thirteen-second conversation before. Maybe with Zach, that one time when he'd found out his son had been hiding a parakeet in his room.

"Get rid of it," Owen had said. "Now."

That was the end of that. Probably five seconds to do that conversation. Zach hadn't been quite the free-thinker he was now.

Owen sighed as he got out of bed, still tired from yesterday. He wanted to take the day off, but three tour groups were arriving today, and they had to rope off a staging area for their luggage and create a special line just for them to check in.

He was busy, busy, busy, and when he thought about

taking a break and heading up to the ninth floor where Gina had been working in the closet, he had to remind himself that she wasn't there.

She didn't call either. Not before dinnertime, and not before Owen made it home and found Cooper had made Belgian waffles and sausage.

"Thanks, bud," he said as he smeared whipped cream on his waffle. "These look way better than last time."

"Yeah, I didn't heat the milk too much, so it didn't kill the yeast."

He gave everything he had to his job and his sons, and as he collapsed in an armchair and stared at whatever Coop had put on the TV, he wondered if he even had room for Gina in his life.

She took up so much of his mental time and energy, and with it being one o'clock in the morning there now, he couldn't call her and ask her how things were going with her business.

As always, Owen had a lot of questions for her, but the biggest one was: Why hadn't she called?

# SEVENTEEN

GINA'S PHONE had ten percent battery life by ten a.m. and she still had tons of business to do with it. She'd arrived in Dallas the previous morning, but all she'd been able to do was confirm that Toni had indeed not been at the office, or the supply warehouse, or her house since Monday.

Then the jet lag had caught up to Gina, and the migraine that started behind her eyes couldn't be ignored. Her house in suburban Dallas felt like a tomb, but she managed to remember where the ibuprofen was located and took enough to knock the headache out. Well, that and a whole lot of sleep.

She'd woken at five o'clock and had been on her phone ever since, texting Toni's friends, getting information about her, the last man she dated, anything she could think of.

No one had seen Toni since Monday night.

Gina's stomach growled, and she got up to take care of herself. She couldn't afford to be back in bed this afternoon.

So she got ready, went into the city to grab breakfast, and then she went to the office.

She'd asked Sammy to pull all their current clients. Anyone with an open job. Anyone on the schedule. Anyone they'd done business with in the past four years.

Gina had spoken with the accountant and asked for a monthly report from the last forty-eight months, and he'd promised he could have them for her by noon today. She arrived at Classy Closets, the entrance and lobby welcoming and comfortable.

She drew in a deep breath. She'd missed this place, missed Dallas, even if she didn't have the same friends here as she had in Hawaii. And the funny thing was, she'd only been in Getaway Bay for six months. She'd lived in Dallas for twelve years.

And of course, there was Owen to consider. She couldn't stop thinking about him, but she couldn't stop to talk to him either. She had to know if Toni had taken anything with her. She had to know where Toni was.

Her desperation had topped the charts before she'd even boarded the plane in Hawaii. So while she felt at home in this lobby, it didn't matter if someone had taken what she'd worked so hard to build.

*How can this be happening again?* she thought, tears springing to her eyes. What did she need to do differently?

*Be here. Be present. Do everything. Trust no one.*

But that was impossible. She couldn't do every job. Manage every account. She'd outgrown what she could handle as a single employee within two years of starting Classy Closets. So how did she find the right people to trust?

She obviously had no idea how to judge character, and it was no wonder she didn't have any friends in Texas.

Pushing her thoughts away so she could focus on the task at hand, she straightened her shoulders and went through the door on the right. Her office had been mostly untouched since she left. The cleaners had obviously been in regularly, but nothing much had changed besides that.

At least that she could see. After Ian had taken so much and left, Gina had hired a data security specialist to help ensure that nothing like what he'd done could happen again. He'd been in Atlanta when she'd called him yesterday, but they had a meeting for later that night.

Just another reason Gina took another bite of her blueberry muffin and a sip of her coffee. She had to be prepared to work all day and into the night.

Troy knocked and lingered in the doorway. "Are you ready for me?" He carried a single file folder that held quite a lot of paper.

"Yes, come in." Gina settled behind her desk and prepared herself though her pulse refused to be quieted. "Lay it on me, Troy."

He took a piece of paper out of the folder and placed it on the desk before sitting across from her. "Good news, ma'am. The accounts are balanced. You're not missing a single dime." He nodded to the paper. "That's the summary. Of course, you can go through it month by month, and that's what these are." He set the folder on the edge of the desk.

Gina picked up the paper and studied it, but she'd gone into interior design and professional organization, not accounting or math. She did like it when numbers matched up, and she could tell that from the sheet that they did.

"Thank you, Troy." She looked up at him. "How long have you been here at Classy Closets?"

"Five years, ma'am." His eyes held knowledge, and while Gina had known he'd been here when the Ian fiasco had happened, she wasn't sure how much longer before that.

"So you don't think Toni's taken any money from us?"

"No, ma'am." Troy cocked his head and studied her.

"What is it?" Gina asked.

"Have we called the police?"

"It's on my to-do list today," Gina said. "And the hospitals." She didn't want Toni to be in trouble or injured, but at the moment, it was the only explanation that wouldn't crush her. "I just…she'd just been promoted. I don't understand." The fear and desperation crept into her voice, and she hated that she'd let her emotions show, especially in front of her accountant.

Someone knocked on her door again, and she switched her attention to the woman there. A petite blonde, Sammy wore really high heels and way too much makeup. But she seemed to know the Classy Closets systems like the back of her hand, despite only starting a couple of months ago.

"Sorry to interrupt, ma'am." She clicked her way forward. "I've compiled names and phone numbers of everyone you requested here." She laid what looked like a packet of papers on the desk. "Full client details can be accessed from here." She placed a thumb drive on the packet. "If you need more than that."

Gina didn't dare touch it. Was she really going to call every client and ask them about Toni? "Thank you, Sammy." Her voice sounded two octaves too low. And she didn't like the sympathetic looks on their faces, but she did appreciate them.

She felt like she was spinning wildly out of control. Her chest tightened, and she couldn't get a decent breath. "I'm —" She couldn't speak. Tears came to her eyes, and she couldn't call them back.

*I'm lost*, she thought. Nothing Doctor White had helped her with could help her now, as she didn't have any control of her thoughts. And Gina hated being out of control.

"Troy, could you go get Miss Jackson some water?"

The man nearly ran from the room, and Sammy followed him, closing the door after he'd left and locking it. Gina wanted her to leave too, but instead, Sammy came around the desk and enveloped her in a tight hug.

"We'll find her," she said. "She must've been very important to you."

Gina wanted to correct her, tell her that while yes, she was worried about Toni, she was really wondering how she could expand her business, get back to Hawaii and Owen, and learn to trust someone with what she couldn't do. She was really crying because she couldn't control this situation, or another person, or pretty much anything.

But she needed an anchor right now, and none of her friends from Getaway Bay were here. So she clung to Sammy and cried until she found an iota of control and seized onto it.

"I'm sorry," she said as she pulled back and wiped her

face. She hadn't put on much more than lip gloss, so at least she didn't have raccoon eyes. "I'm just so tired." Tired was the perfect way to put it, and not just physically. Physical exhaustion she could cure. This level of tired—her emotional, mental, and spiritual exhaustion—she didn't know how to fix.

"It's fine, ma'am." Sammy looked at her with compassion. "What would you like me to do next?"

"It's Saturday, Sammy. Don't you have somewhere else to be?"

"Not if you need me here."

Gina looked at the thumb drive. "I think I'm going to start with the police," she said. "And then call some hospitals. Maybe could you grab your phone and help with that?"

"Sure thing, ma'am. I'll be right back." She left the office, and Gina felt the oxygen in the air go with her.

They worked through the afternoon with few results. No unidentified people had been brought into a hospital in the past five days, and a pair of officers came over from the police department and asked dozens of questions, took copies of the financial reports, contacts, and the same list of people Gina had already contacted.

Her data security expert texted to say the flights through Chicago were grounded, and he wouldn't be able to make it to Dallas, and by the time darkness fell, Gina felt like she'd worked for hours and gotten nowhere.

She went home, but there was nothing for her there. Emptiness. Loneliness. Darkness. Standing in the kitchen, the glow of the clock on the stove the only light, she understood why she'd left to pursue the inkling of a possibility to work on the closets at Stacey's bed and breakfast.

She thought of the women she spent time with on the beach, and she knew they'd be there for her if she called them. *They're busy,* was her first thought.

*So what?* was her second.

She picked up her phone and called the emergency number for Doctor White. "Gina," she answered on the second ring. "Tell me what's going on."

Gina really liked that Doctor White never asked questions. She just wanted to open every conversation with "tell me."

"My general manager hasn't been to work in five days," she said. "I'm freaking out."

"Okay, take a step back from that panic."

Gina tried, but she felt like she'd been transported to a foreign land. "I'm in Texas."

"Okay, Texas is fine, Gina. Tell me where you are."

"I'm standing in my house in Dallas."

"Dallas is good. You've told me great things about Dallas. Tell me about the weather."

"It's nighttime. I think it was sunny today. It's snowing in Chicago." Numbness spread through Gina, but at least she wasn't about to punch the wall.

Doctor White continued to talk to her, and after a few minutes, Gina felt like she could finally say what she'd called to say. "I want to call someone to come help me," she whispered. "But I don't trust anyone. I don't trust myself to know who to call. Life is so much easier when I don't need help. When I can just rely on myself." She stopped before she said everything, like how her company had never abandoned her. Never made her go from home to home. Never asked more of her than she wanted to give.

"Everyone needs help," Doctor White said. "You called me for help. Tell me who you want in your apartment with you, making coffee for you so you can sleep a few more minutes, bringing you something to eat so you don't forget."

"Owen."

"What did he say when you asked him to come?"

Gina couldn't say anything.

"Tell me you've asked him."

"I haven't spoken to him yet," Gina said, her blurting taking center stage. "I said I'd call him, but I haven't. When he called, I was rushed. I—I don't know if I have room for him in my life."

"There's so much here to unpack," Doctor White said. "We can deal with it another time. I'm immediately concerned about you being alone. Is there anyone you feel comfortable asking for help?"

Gina said, "My friend, Lexie. She lives in Hawaii. She'd probably come."

"It's not about who'll come, Gina. Owen would come. It's about who you feel comfortable *asking for help*. Who you trust."

"I don't trust anyone."

"Again, that's something we can work on at another time. I don't want you to be alone tonight. Lexie's here in Hawaii. Anyone you can get to tonight?"

"No." Gina's voice barely left her mouth.

"Then I'll call you every hour," Doctor White said. "If you don't answer, I will call the police."

Tears streamed down Gina's face. She nodded, but of course, Doctor White couldn't see that.

"I need you to verbally agree to have me call you every hour," Doctor White said, her normally calm voice stern.

"Okay," Gina said. "I'll answer."

"Thank you," Doctor White said. "I have one more request. Please call Owen. Right now, as soon as you hang up with me."

"Okay," Gina said. Their call ended, and she gripped her phone until she felt sure the plastic would crack.

Then she dialed Lexie.

# EIGHTEEN

OWEN'S PHONE RANG, but it wasn't as loud as usual. He searched his desk for the device, not seeing it. "Where is it?" He pushed his chair back and searched the floor. There, a flash of light between the two pieces of his desk unit.

He stretched for it, but he seemed to be moving in slow motion. He touched the phone right when it stopped ringing, and his fingers scrabbled along the smooth surface, trying to get it to slide out.

Finally, he got it and straightened, a groan leaking out of his mouth. "Gina."

He jammed his finger on the *call* button, hoping she'd pick up. Praying.

When she said, "Owen," in a broken voice, he shot to standing.

"Gina, what's going on there?" He didn't care how he sounded. She was in distress, and he hated with everything in him that he'd stayed on the island when he should've gone with her to Dallas.

"Nothing's going on." She sniffed. "I've been here a couple of days, and it feels like we've done a lot, with no results."

"So you haven't found your general manager?"

"Not yet."

"What do you need?"

"I'm doing okay."

"Gina...." She obviously wasn't okay. He wanted to tell her about the strained couple of days with his kids, but he couldn't. He wanted to ask her more questions, but he was afraid of driving her away.

"I'm not missing any money," she said. "No clients. But Toni's just gone. Poof. Gone."

"So hire someone else." Owen regretted the words as soon as they left his mouth.

"It's not that simple," Gina said. "Where is Toni? Why did she leave without saying anything? She worked here for years and years. How can I replace her with someone I trust?"

Gina sounded completely out of control, and Owen had no idea what to do. "I'll come," he said. "I'll help you."

"Lexie is already on her way."

"What?" The word exploded out of Owen.

"I called Lexie. She has a jet at the airport there. She'll be in the air within the hour."

"You called Lexie." The disbelief in Owen's voice boomed in his own ears.

"You're busy."

"So is Lexie." Owen had so much more to say. "Besides, that's what people do for those they care about. They make sacrifices. I would've come, Gina." He still had half a mind to go anyway. He wondered how far away that would drive Gina.

When she didn't say anything, Owen decided now was as good of time as any to lay his cards on the table. "I care about you," he said. "I don't know why that scares you so much, but I know it does. You won't let me in. I'm been standing at the door for months, Gina. Knocking. Begging. Trying. *You* have to let me in. You have—" His voice quit, and that had never happened to him before. Even when he was angry with Zach, he'd managed to have the hard conversations. Even with difficult guests, he kept his cool.

But Gina had unraveled every part of him, and still she wouldn't take down the invisible wall between them.

Fisher entered his office, took one look at Owen, and held up his hand. "I'll come back," he mouthed and backed into the hall, the door closing again.

Owen didn't know what else to say, and Gina was certainly staying silent.

She finally said, "I have to stay here for a while. I don't know when I'll be back to work on the closets."

"I don't care about the closets."

"I'll call you later."

Owen couldn't believe the words in his mind, that he let them come out of his mouth. "You know what, Gina? I'll make things easier for you. You don't need to call me. Seems like you have plenty of other *friends* to rely on. I want more than that. More than the billionaire's boyfriend.

More than call you later. I want you to trust *me*, confide in *me*, rely on *me*, no matter how busy you think I am." He couldn't breathe, and the thoughts in his head spun like a tornado.

"And you're not ready to do that. Okay, fine. Call me when you are." He wanted to hang up, but he wasn't a petulant fifteen-year-old.

But his heart was taking a beating, and not in the normal way. She crushed him when she said, "Okay," and hung up.

He pulled the phone from his ear and looked at it. The call had definitely been disconnected.

Anger and disappointment roared through Owen. He wanted to call Lexie and yell at her for agreeing to go to Texas without him. Wanted to throw his phone in one of the industrial washing machines so when Gina did call him again, he wouldn't have to put his heart on the line again. Wanted to leave Getaway Bay for a while, until he could figure out how to live here without her.

Instead, he stood, buttoned his suit jacket, and opened his door. Fisher loitered down the hall, his head bent over his phone. "I'm ready, Fisher," he said, his voice an alien version of normal, but Owen felt like that from head to toe, so he couldn't expect his voice to be right.

Fisher turned, concern in his face. "Gina's in Texas?"

"I'm not talking about Gina," Owen growled. "If you have business to discuss, please come in."

"So you're not going to Dallas?"

Owen turned and went back into his office, almost slamming the door behind him. But loud noises scared the fish, so he didn't. Plus, he didn't want to act like an emotional idiot in front of his boss, even if Fisher was also his best friend.

"Did you two break up?" Fisher came in and closed the door, obviously not giving up on talking about Gina.

"Yes," Owen clipped out. "And Zach has a girlfriend of eight months he didn't tell me about, and I found them in his room—alone—yesterday, and he's going to the University of Hawaii." Owen glared. "Can we talk about Sweet Breeze?"

Fisher unbuttoned his jacket and sat down. "I just came to see how you were doing. It's been a while since we've talked." He gazed evenly at Owen, concern in his eyes but completely composed. "Obviously. Want to start with Zach?"

Owen didn't want to start at all. But he didn't have a therapist like his son or Gina, and he felt like he might explode if he didn't unload. So he started with the college application to UCLA he hadn't known about and went through the last couple of months from there.

An hour later, Owen felt like he'd just wrung out his soul. "So you're in love with her," Fisher said.

From everything Owen had said, that was what he'd gotten? Owen didn't know what to say. "I need to get back to work." He turned toward his computer, but he had no idea what task he'd been doing before Gina had called.

In fact, he couldn't remember what his life had been like before the beautiful brunette had waltzed into it.

He knew it hadn't been as vibrant. As fun. As exhilarating. In fact, Owen had just been putting in time. He hadn't been living.

And he wanted to live.

"Let me and Stacey take the boys for a few days."

"Why?" Owen asked. "So I can drown in my misery alone? I can handle the boys. They're not the problem."

"No, I suppose not." Fisher tilted his head as if he knew Owen was just staring at the computer screen—which was still dark. "You've always done great with them, Owen."

"I suppose. Nothing harder or easier than other parents." He just had to do everything alone.

*Alone.*

He was so tired of being alone. Even surrounded by people, even with Fisher sitting five feet across from him, Owen felt all alone.

His phone rang again, and he had no choice but to see who was calling. "It's Lexie."

"Maybe she wants you to go with her."

"I'm not going." He swiped the call to voicemail too. "And I'm not talking to her."

"Why not?"

"She's more your friend. And Gina's." Owen didn't mean to sound bitter. He wasn't, not really. Fisher had his little club, and Owen's bank account wasn't big enough for it.

"Is this about the Nine-0 Club?" Fisher had some of the same intuition others had credited to Owen.

"Of course not. I know you have your thing. I'm just saying, I can't even remember the last time I talked to Lexie. I'm surprised she even has my number."

"Hmm."

"What?"

"Don't you want to go to Gina?"

"Yes," Owen said in a quick explosion of breath. "Yes, Fisher, okay? Yes, I'm in love with her, and yes, I'd get on a plane and fly there right now. If—if she *wanted* me to. And she doesn't." His chest heaved as the truth of his words cleaved through his whole body. "She doesn't want me."

———

A day passed, and the pain in Owen's heart didn't lessen. A week went by without word from anyone—not Gina, not Lexie, not Fisher. Owen was actually glad for the first time in his life that there were more visitors in Getaway Bay than residents.

He didn't care how much they drank, either. Or if the Wi-Fi went down. In fact, he was considering handing out two-for-one coupons at the bar and cutting the Internet lines himself. That way, he'd have something to keep his mind off the woman who'd sailed into Hawaii, stolen his heart, and then disappeared.

Zach kept to the rules, and Maizee started hanging out at the house more often. Owen liked her, but he could see why Zach wasn't serious about her. They took their AP tests and settled in for the last month of school.

Zach agreed to a few graduation pictures, and they sent out announcements with his commencement and where he'd be attending college in the fall.

"What about Mom?" Zach asked as Owen put the last stamp on an envelope.

Owen glanced at his son. "You want to send her one?" He abandoned the task of searching for another sheet of stamps. "Zach, she won't come. I'm not even sure where she is."

His son's face stayed passive, a complete mask. "I know. She should still know I'm graduating." He looked at Owen, a perfect storm of emotions in his eyes. "Don't you think?"

"Sure," Owen said. "I'll find out where she is and send her an announcement." Things moved on after that, but Owen really didn't want to text Linda and get her address. Maybe he could just send her a picture of the announcement and be done with it.

Cooper finished the basketball season with great stats, and he started coming over to the hotel to work out after school, just to stay in shape until tryouts next year.

Owen worked, sent the text to his ex-wife, slept, and managed to eat when his body told him to. His phone only chimed or rang when there was a problem, and he really missed his fun, flirtatious text sessions with Gina.

One time, he wandered up to the eighth floor, to the last apartment-suite she'd been working on. Though the plumber, electrician, and painters had all been in the room, the closet still held a hint of Gina's fruity, feminine scent. He stood in the space she loved so much, and allowed himself to love her for just a moment.

Then the agony of not having her took over, and Owen spun away from the island she'd gushed about and left the room.

With only two weeks until graduation and a huge change in Owen's life, Stacey called him.

"Hey," she said.

"I'm not talking about Gina," Owen said, peering at a

piece of paper in front of him and trying to make the numbers line up with a spreadsheet on his monitor. He really needed reading glasses, and the thought that he was almost fifty hit him square in the gut.

"It's not about Gina," Stacey said. "I'm wondering if you want to take me to a movie while Fisher does his...meeting thing. Whatever."

Owen abandoned his work, the bitterness and jealousy in Stacey's voice intriguing him. "You're not invited to his little club?"

"I only have seven zeroes in my bank account. And I happen to know you do too, and I figured we had enough money to blow it on overpriced popcorn and a box of stale candy."

Owen couldn't help the laugh that burst from his mouth. He hadn't laughed in so long, the sound felt strange coming from him. Even the fish seemed a bit startled.

"I'm in," he said. "When is this *special meeting*?"

"Tomorrow at one-thirty. I know that's close to check-in, but—"

"I don't care. I'm in." And the boys would still be at school, and Owen just wanted to get away from himself and his life for a while.

"Perfect, I'll meet you in the lobby at one."

The next day, Owen left his office a few minutes before he needed to meet Stacey. As he rounded the corner to enter the lobby, he ran straight into a very solid body.

Jason.

Owen had managed to avoid Jason over the past several weeks by pretending to be engrossed in a text conversation when he walked by, or giving the check-in counter a wide berth as he came out of the hall, or simply waiting to leave his office until he knew the security guard would have rotated to his next post.

But he couldn't avoid him now.

"Hey, Owen," he said easily, as if his wife hadn't chartered her private jet to go save Owen's girlfriend.

"Hey, Jason." Owen tried to move away, but a large group of tourists pressed in on him, keeping him sandwiched next to Jason.

"Lexie came home," he said, his eyes flitting around, never quite settling on Owen.

"Really?" Owen didn't want to leave now. He had some strange pull to know about Gina even though he'd done everything he could to ignore her.

Honestly, it hadn't been hard. She hadn't texted or called, and avoiding a single security guard was solidly inside Owen's skill set.

"Yeah, got home last night," he said. "She hasn't said much, but I can keep my ears open." He didn't say, "if you want," but it was implied, especially when he finally did meet Owen's eyes with an edge of anxiety in his.

"I'm fine, Jason. Thank you. I'm glad your wife is home safely." He made to button his jacket, realizing too late that he'd left it in his office. Without that gesture to fall back on, Owen didn't know what to do with his hands.

"Yeah, thanks." Jason looked a bit perplexed, but the crowd shifted, and Owen took his opportunity to slip away. Stacey waited over by a pillar, and Owen approached her.

"You ready?"

She wore what was clearly a swimming suit cover up, flip flops, and her hair in a floppy bun on top of her head. She looked like she'd just come in from the beach for a drink, not like she'd be going to a movie with him.

"Yeah, ready." She flashed him a smile, but he could already tell she was distracted.

"We don't have to go."

Her eyes met his, and he saw in an instant that she didn't want to go. "I want to, Owen," she said. "I really do, but the girls are out on the beach...."

"And Lexie's home." Owen nodded toward the doorway across the lobby, past the restaurant, that would take Stacey back to the beach. Back to her friends. Back to the gossip.

"Go on."

"Really?"

"I'll be fine." He didn't need a babysitter, though he had been looking forward to the movie with Stacey. At least for a couple of hours, maybe he wouldn't feel like someone had cut him out of his own life and pasted him into an alternate version of it.

Stacey flung her arms around him and said, "Thank you, Owen," before hurrying off in the direction of the beach.

Owen watched her go, wishing the lump in his throat wasn't quite so big. Wishing he didn't feel like such a loser. Wishing he had friends to rush off to as well.

# NINETEEN

GINA OPENED the fridge to find a big bag of the omelet muffins Lexie had made for her. She mourned the loss of having a friend so close, but Lexie had stayed for just over a month. She had a life back on the island, and she couldn't stay forever.

Gina, however, felt like she'd been sentenced to a life of loneliness, and it was completely unsatisfying.

After all, her closeting systems couldn't share the excitement of landing a big client. Her tool belt didn't want to take her to dinner to talk to her. Her empty house didn't get fuller just because Gina bought more furniture.

And while she hadn't thought she wanted someone to talk to, to ask her questions, to share her life with, now that she'd had even a brief taste of it with Owen, she found everything else in her life lacking.

She keyed in the code at the mansion where she'd been

working for the past week and called, "Hello? It's Gina from Classy Closets."

No one answered, and Gina went in and closed the door behind her. She hadn't expected anyone to be home, as she'd been working in the house alone for days.

And if there was any building on earth that felt emptier than her house, it was this one. The people obviously had plenty of money. The best of everything. But there wasn't a single photo on the walls. No evidence of love or friendship in their lives. It was almost like she was organizing and designing for a robot.

But apparently robots could afford to pay for expensive closeting systems, so Gina got to work.

Work.

It seemed to be the only thing she had in her life that was constant. She'd spoken to Doctor White on the phone weekly while Lexie had been here, but if she wasn't going to return to Getaway Bay, Gina knew she should probably go back to her therapist here.

The problem was, Gina hadn't decided fully to stay in Dallas.

Toni had finally turned up in Washington D.C., where an old college roommate lived. She'd had a drinking problem and her friend had convinced her to come home with her and start a treatment program.

"The only way I could get her to come was to leave right then," Iris had explained. "I thought she'd at least call."

Well, she hadn't. But she also hadn't taken anything, destroyed client files, or done anything else even remotely close to what Ian had done.

And still, Gina couldn't get herself to pick up the phone and talk to Owen. Every time she thought about him, embarrassment and humiliation tore through her.

It had taken a few weeks until she'd realized what she'd done to him by not asking him to come be at her side in her hour of greatest need. She knew that was all he'd wanted, and she'd denied him.

Apologizing now felt weak. Nowhere good enough for such a great guy as Owen. Lexie had tried to get her to come back with her, claiming Owen would understand.

But Gina didn't think so. He had made it easy for her to forget about him, move on with her life, but what he didn't get was that she'd never forget him and never move past him.

"So what are you going to do?" she asked the screwdriver she held as she lifted it to tighten a piece of hardware holding a shelf.

She couldn't even answer her own question. With Toni gone, Gina didn't have anyone to run the company, so she'd determined to stay until she hired someone new.

But she hadn't even posted the job anywhere. She was doing it, because then she knew it would get done right.

But her heart wasn't in this closet, or this house. Still, she hammered and hung, worked and worried, until it was time to go home.

Lexie texted just as Gina picked up a sandwich for dinner, saying she'd made it back to the island and asking how Gina's first day alone was.

*Great*, Gina sent, because it hadn't been bad. She'd have

to make new standards for things, as great in Texas wasn't anywhere near what great had been in Hawaii.

She ate the sandwich though it tasted a couple of days old, and she checked her schedule for the following day. The only difference between tonight and the last few weeks was that Lexie hadn't ordered dinner, hadn't filled the nighttime hours with chatter and conversation, and hadn't been available for Gina to confess her worries to.

The silence was somewhat comforting, but Gina knew now that she preferred the company of another person over being stuck inside her own mind.

*Have you seen Owen?* she asked Lexie.

*No, I just got home. Nine-0 tomorrow afternoon, though. I'll see if I can't run into him.*

Gina's chest collapsed at the mention of the Nine-0 Club. While she'd never really felt like she fit in, she had enjoyed going to the events, meeting new people, and having a place to belong.

"Having a place to belong," she said aloud. That was what she'd wanted her entire life. A family to belong to. A home where she belonged.

At first, she'd worked for that, but after the fourth placement, she'd realized that she'd be moved around until she turned eighteen. She didn't belong anywhere.

Her control slipped, and Gina refocused her thoughts the way Doctor White had taught her. Within a few seconds, she felt like herself—or whatever this new version of herself was.

With a jolt, Gina realized that she had two selves. One that lived here in Dallas, wallowing in her past and how awful it had been. One who wished she had someone to trust at work, someone to help her run this Texas headquarters of Classy Closets.

And she had a self who'd thrived on the tropical beaches of Hawaii. Who'd done the jobs required to get the reputation she wanted. Who'd fallen in love with a handsome man, even though she'd kept him at arm's length for months.

"I can't stay in Texas," she said to the half-eaten sandwich. It, of course, did not answer back.

*Do you think Owen would forgive me?* Gina texted to Lexie.

*Of course he will.*

*I need to do something big to apologize.*

*I think Owen would like the opposite of that, actually.*

But Gina needed to do it. Needed him to know that for him, she'd do whatever it took to get him back.

*Any ideas?*

*Let me talk to Jason. He knows Owen pretty well.*

Gina relaxed back into the couch, her mind whirring in a good way for the first time in weeks. She'd done plenty of thinking while she got caught up to speed on everything happening in the Dallas office, while she sorted through Toni's desk, and while she'd contemplated her next move.

"The job," she said, practically lunging for her laptop. The sooner she hired a new general manager, the sooner she could get back to Getaway Bay and start planting roots. Roots that would get exactly what they needed under the hot sun and the tender care of Owen Church.

———

Two weeks later, Gina's plane landed just as the stars started to wink to life in the sky. Perfect. Owen wouldn't be at the hotel, and the only way he'd know she was back on the island was if he had a watch put on her name at Sweet Breeze.

She very much doubted that he had done such a thing.

"Welcome back, Miss Jackson," the man at the check-in counter said, and Gina took the key from him to the fifth-floor long-term apartment suite.

Once inside, Gina marveled at the elegance of it, the functionality not suffering because of the gleaming stainless steel appliances and marble flooring in the bathroom.

Though it was getting late, she pulled up the real estate listings she practically had memorized. Tomorrow, she'd have to employ a spy or two to get out of the hotel without Owen knowing, but she had complete faith in her friends.

*Friends.*

Gina sighed as she sat on the couch, just being back in Getaway Bay more soothing than she'd even imagined. This place called to her soul and helped her feel like she'd returned to where she belonged.

The next day, she toured the ten-thousand square foot space, liking the huge windows that overlooked the east bay.

"I think it's big enough," she said to Lexie, who had come with her for the real estate tours. "What do you think?"

"It's just you for now, right?"

"Right. So plenty of space to store the systems, put a desk, that kind of thing." Gina turned in a circle, her heart

SWEET BREEZE RESORT 193

lighter than it had been since that fateful phone call almost two months ago.

"I won't be working here much," she said. "The job at Sweet Breeze is months from conclusion."

"Still would be nice to have a place to do business," Lexie said. "I think this is the one."

They'd looked at three other commercial properties that day, and Gina nodded. "You're right. This is the one."

The real estate agent beamed at them. "So we'll offer on this one?"

Gina grinned, the gesture a bit foreign on her face but satisfying too. "Yes, put an offer in on this. Asking price is fine. I think it's fair."

"It's fair," Scott confirmed. "And we still have time to get to that first house today, if you'd like to."

Gina met Lexie's eye. "You game?"

"Absolutely." Lexie followed Scott and Gina into the hallway. "When are you planning on telling Owen you're back?"

"A couple more days," Gina said vaguely. She had a plan, but she didn't want to tell anyone quite yet.

Well, she had to tell two people, and after she and Lexie went through a cute house on the beach, she said good-bye to her friend and headed down the sand to a snow-cone shack.

Her heart thundered in her chest, especially when the two teenage boys came into view. "Hey, guys," she said, causing both of them to turn. "Should we order first?" She hooked her thumb toward the shack. "Talk while we eat?"

"All right," Cooper said, shooting his older brother a nervous look.

"We can talk while we wait in line," Zach said, reminding Gina so much of Owen that she laughed.

"Fair enough," she said. "Look, I don't know what your dad has been like, but I'm going to try to make it up to him."

"How?" Zach asked, the doubt still very much alive in his eyes.

"I'll need your help," she said, eyeing the menu and wondering what in the world tiger's blood tasted like. "And I wanted to run this by you, because it has to do with you as well."

"Me?" Zach's eyebrows shot toward his hairline.

"Yeah. Aren't you graduating on Thursday?"

# TWENTY

OWEN KNOTTED and then re-knotted his son's tie. Finally Zach swatted his hands away. "I got this, Dad. Go see what Cooper needs." It was a polite way for Zach to tell Owen to get lost.

He left his older son's room and went next door to Cooper's. He wasn't sure what he was so nervous about. Zach was going to graduate—with honors, no less. They had the cords and everything.

But Zach had told him last night that he wanted to move out over the summer. Get a job and live on his own. Owen had nodded and smiled and asked questions. Zach seemed to know what he wanted. He thought through everything privately and only came to Owen once the decision had been made.

Owen liked that and didn't at the same time. He'd like to be more involved in helping his son make such huge life choices, but then he reminded himself that Zach seemed to be doing fine on his own.

For some reason, Owen felt like another bomb was about to drop, and he had no idea what Zach would do next.

"Hey, bud," he said to Cooper, who sat on the bed, his head bent to look at his phone. "Are you ready?"

Cooper looked up, his expression glazed over for a moment. "Yeah. I'm ready." His tie was perfectly knotted, and as he stood, Owen realized how tall he'd gotten. How broad his shoulders now spanned, and how muscular he'd become. Cooper had two years of high school left, but he was rapidly becoming a man.

Owen smiled at him, soft emotions racing through him. What would Cooper do with his life? Would he stay nearby or go somewhere far away?

What would Owen do once his sons didn't need him anymore?

He pushed the troubling thoughts away and swept his fingers along Cooper's hairline, though not a single hair sat out of place. "Big day for Zach."

"Yeah, he's nervous about—" Cooper cut off, but Owen heard something there.

He cocked his head. "About what?"

"Moving on." Cooper wasn't a very good liar, so at least Owen had that as comfort.

"He's ready for that," Owen said, wanting to push the issue. But he decided that he'd find out soon enough. After all, if Zach was nervous about something, it would have to happen soon, right?

So Owen stepped back and said, "It's time to go,"

watching Cooper as he moved into the hall. They found Zach in the kitchen, a handful of chocolate covered macadamia nuts in his hand.

Definitely nervous.

Zach ate when he was trying to calm down, and Cooper starved himself. Owen brought his sons together and put one arm around each of their shoulders.

They huddled together, the way they'd been doing for a decade now. "I love you guys," Owen said, his emotion catching in his throat.

"Love you too, Dad," Cooper said in unison with Zach.

Owen drew in a deep breath. "All right. We better go. Don't want to be late." He stepped out of the huddle, sensing that from this moment on, his life would be different. He'd have to figure out how to parent an adult child, as if this parenting thing hadn't already been hard enough.

"You're driving yourself?" he asked Zach, who nodded. "You want to go with him or me?" he asked Cooper.

"I'll go with him." He obviously knew things would be different after today—well, after Zach moved away to college—and another wave of emotion swept over him as Zach slung his arm around Cooper's shoulders and they headed for the garage together.

How could Linda not be here for this? Owen didn't understand his ex-wife or her decision to remove herself from something so precious to Owen. She'd responded to his text with the picture of Zach's graduation announcement with *Tell him congratulations! I'll send him something.* Nothing had come yet, and Owen wasn't holding his breath every time he checked the mail.

For one irrational moment, he thought about texting Gina. Just something simple like *I miss you,* so she'd know she could come back to him whenever she was ready.

Owen just seriously doubted she'd *ever* be ready.

He drove over to the basketball arena where the graduation was being held. He wasn't late, but the parking lot was filling rapidly. He parked, texted Cooper to pick a spot to sit in and let him know.

His son came back with *Fisher and Stacey are in section E, row 11. I'll head there.*

*Perfect. See you there.* Owen texted Fisher to make sure there were enough seats, but he didn't doubt there would be. Fisher could probably get them seats on the stage if that was what Owen wanted.

He smiled at the thought and started the long walk inside. Thankfully, the air conditioners in the convention center were operating at full capacity, and by the time Owen sat down beside Cooper, he wasn't sweating anymore.

He glanced down the row at Fisher and Stacey, and said, "Thanks for saving the seats." He noticed at least eight more past Stacey. "Who else is coming?"

"Everyone," Fisher said. "Tyler and Tawny. Esther and Marshall. Lexie and Jason. Sasha and Jasper. Lawrence. Ira and Gabi." He turned and counted the seats, his finger bobbing with each one. "Someone else. Who did I miss?"

"Sterling," Stacey said, fanning herself with the program.

Owen was touched at the outpouring of support for him and his son. "So I guess the dinner at Aloha Hideaway will cost me more than I thought, huh?"

"Nope. I knew how many had RSVP'ed." Stacey smiled

at him and rested one hand on her stomach. Owen immediately knew something was going on with her, and he suspected she was pregnant.

A smile touched his lips, but he turned away before Fisher or Stacey noticed. "My dad should be here soon." He checked his phone to see if his father had texted. Not yet.

"Oh, he came over from Oahu?" Fisher asked.

"Yeah, last night." Owen's father was old, almost ninety, and the fact that he'd gotten on a plane to come to Zach's graduation was a very big deal. "He wouldn't stay at my place," he said. "Despite my guest bedroom."

Fisher shook his head. "Yeah, he's at Sweet Breeze. I told him the shuttle would bring him over any time."

Tyler arrived then with Tawny, Jasper, Sasha, Lexie, and Jason.

Owen stood and gave handshakes and hugs, even to Lexie, who he still hadn't spoken with since her return from Dallas.

She seemed a little nervous as she skirted past him to an empty seat down the row. But she'd come, and that meant a lot to Owen.

He glanced around the floor below them, where the graduates would march in and sit.

"Did Zach tell you which side he was coming in on?" he asked Cooper, but he couldn't answer before Owen's dad arrived.

"Dad, you made it." Owen hugged his father, and Fisher and Stacey moved down to make room for him.

Owen did all the introductions, just finished when Esther and Marshall showed up. Esther carried their baby girl on her hip, and she seemed so floppy to Owen. Still, he cooed at baby Ella and let them move down the row. Esther immediately passed the baby to Stacey, who bounced her on her lap like she knew exactly what to do with an infant.

The music started and the first people came out of the doors on either side of the stage that had been set up. Section E had a fabulous view of the stage and both lines of graduates, and Owen eagerly waited for Zach to make an appearance.

But he didn't. And didn't. With a last name that started with C, he should've been near the front.

Owen frowned when at least half the graduates had come out and flipped open his program, just to make sure his son was graduating today.

If that was the secret he and Cooper had been keeping.... Owen's heart flopped uselessly in his chest.

But he found Zach's name in the list and glanced back up. "Did I miss him?" he whispered to Cooper.

"He hasn't come out yet," Cooper said, unconcerned.

Around him, families cheered for their graduate while Owen's frustration grew.

Almost every chair was full now.

The orchestra started on one more round of pomp and circumstance, and the principal of the school came out of the tunnel, followed by a few faculty members and then more green-robed students.

He climbed the stairs to the stage, the line of people behind him doing the same thing.

Owen sucked in a breath when he saw Zach going up those stairs.

"What in the world?"

"Did you even look at your program?" Fisher asked, his voice full of teasing.

But Owen couldn't look now, because he was too busy soaking in the bright yellow cords that signified his son was graduating with honors.

Not only that, he wore a white sash over his shoulders, which made a V in front on his chest.

"He's the valedictorian," Owen said, pure wonder in his voice. He turned to Cooper. "Is that what you guys weren't telling me?"

"He wanted it to be a surprise," Cooper said, his face a full smile as he applauded.

Fisher whooped and Tyler yelled Zach's name. He looked up to them and waved, his face so full of joy Owen wanted to cry.

Instead, he pulled his emotions back and waved at his son. His son, the valedictorian.

"He'll have a speech." Owen flipped open the program again, this time madly searching the other side for the order of things.

Sure enough, there was Zach's name about halfway down. "So he was nervous about his speech." He shook his head, wanting to be angry at his son but not quite pulling it off.

The song ended and everyone sat, and now Owen's nerves turned to what Zach might say during his speech.

The choir sang, and a few faculty members spoke, then the senior class president, who also introduced Zach as the next speaker.

Finally, his son stood at the microphone, and Owen could see his nerves from way across the stadium floor.

"Well, here we are," Zach said, a smile coming across his face and entering his tone. "Once I knew I was the valedictorian and would have to speak to you today, I thought a lot about what I might say. It was hard, because I know some of us are leaving the island. Some of us are staying. Some of us have parents and grandparents and friends here, and some don't. And what qualifies me to give a speech at all? Just because I got A's doesn't mean I'm anyone special, with something important to say."

He swallowed, and Owen could barely contain the raging river of emotions rolling through him. So much happiness. So much change.

"Then I thought – what would my dad say to you?" Zach continued. "And everything fell into place. See, my dad, he's raised me and my brother all alone for a long time." Zach's face crumpled for a single moment. If Owen hadn't been staring intently at him, he would've missed it.

"He didn't give up when things got hard. Most of the time, he didn't even get mad when things went wrong, or when my brother and I didn't follow the rules. He's always worked hard to make sure we have what we need to be happy. And he never missed anything, despite his busy schedule. This year, my brother was a starter on the basketball team, and my dad attended every single game. Every one."

Zach surveyed the crowd. "I have a point to this, I swear."

People chuckled and twittered, but Owen's heart was beating so loud he could barely hear them.

"A few months ago, he started dating someone," Zach said, and Owen almost flew out of his seat. What was his son doing?

"I wasn't sure what to make of it," Zach said. "He'd never dated before. I thought he was happy, but watching him with her and seeing him come alive again…I didn't really know what happiness was. Her name's Gina, and she grew up in rough circumstances. No family support, because she was in foster care. But she graduated from high school and went on to get two college degrees. And I thought about what my dad would say about her." Zach looked right at Owen now, and Owen leaned forward, not wanting to miss a single syllable.

"He'd say she was smart for looking past her circumstances. That she changed a rough situation into something positive through hard work." Zach looked away, glancing around the crowd again.

"So my point is this: No matter who you are and what kind of grades you got in high school, no matter if you have a big crowd here to support you or no one at all, we can all learn from people like my dad and Gina. Don't give up. Work hard. Be smart and look to the future with hope. Don't get mad when things don't go your way. Find a different solution. Dig in. Show up, and be there." Zach's voice broke on the last word. "Be there for each other."

The crowd started to clap, and the applause grew and grew into something monstrous. Some people stood, and Owen joined them.

Zach stayed at the podium, obviously not finished yet. Once the applause died down, he said, "My dad's not perfect, just in case some of you think he is. But he's taught me a lot about hard work, perseverance, and being there. So if you have someone like that in your life, thank them today. If you don't, be that person for someone else. I just wanted to say thanks to my dad for sticking around and being there, and to Fisher and Stacey DuPont, who sometimes picked up the slack when my dad couldn't. And I hope my dad will once again prove that he's the kind of man who will work through rough things."

Zach turned to his right, and Owen followed his gaze, his heart stopping at the sight of that streaked dark brown hair.

"No," he said.

"I'd like to invite Gina up, who has a few things to say as well. Thank you." Zach stepped back from the microphone as more applause filled the arena.

Gina wore a navy blue dress with sleeves to her elbow. The silver jewelry and loads of makeup couldn't erase her absolute terror.

"Did you know she was back?" Fisher asked, and Owen shook his head.

"What's she going to say?" Stacey asked.

Owen had no idea. He wanted to leave, but couldn't even move a single muscle. Down the row, his friends twittered about Gina's sudden appearance on the island, and the crowd quieted when she leaned forward to speak into the mic.

# TWENTY-ONE

GINA'S HEART would surely explode at any moment. Though Zach's graduating class was only two hundred and eighty people, she felt like she was standing in front of millions.

*Only one matters*, she told herself. She knew where Owen was sitting. The man was like the sun to her soul, always pulling her in with his huge gravitational force.

She didn't dare look to her left, instead deciding to focus her words in the center to the students.

"Hello," she said, glad when the microphone didn't squeal. "I'm grateful to Zach for giving me a few minutes of his speech time today. Honestly, I think he was relieved when I texted him."

The crowd laughed, and Gina relaxed a little. "Isn't he a great kid? Such wise words. While I didn't think I was doing anything extraordinary at the time, he sure made me sound good." She smiled, getting only a few chuckles now. People just wanted to see their student walk across the stage. So Gina got right to the point with, "I think that's how most things in life are. We don't realize how hard something is until we're through it. We don't understand how important something is until it's over. We don't realize how extraordinary we are until the crisis has passed."

She looked at the students. "So take on important things. Be extraordinary. And most of all, when you do something wrong, own it and apologize for it."

Her eyes went to Owen, who wore a look halfway between hope and hate. "That's why I'm here today. See, I did something wrong, and I need to apologize for it. I started a relationship with a great man when *I* wasn't ready for it. I hurt him, and his kids. I left without talking to him. And I put my job above my heart. So today, in front of all these people, I just want to say I'm sorry, Owen. I don't deserve a second chance, but maybe you'll find it in your heart to give me one anyway."

He didn't so much as twitch or move. Gina's heart couldn't take the stormy look on his face for another moment, so she turned her focus down the row of people with him.

"That's all I needed to say. I'm sorry, and I hope anyone I've hurt can forgive me." She stepped back from the microphone, gave Zach a big hug, and hurried down the steps as fast as her heels would carry her.

Behind her, the program went on, the band setting up to play something.

Gina needed to get out of this arena as fast as possible. Get back to the apartment she'd rented while she waited for the house she'd bought to go through some basic renovations and repairs.

Her phone bleeped out a notification she hadn't heard in a while, and she knew it was Owen. She almost didn't dare look to see what he'd said.

She did anyway, because she was going to take Zach's advice and do hard things. Show up and be there.

*Where are you?*

She didn't want to tell him she was leaving, because he wouldn't be able to follow. Surely he wanted to see his oldest son graduate.

*Headed back to my apartment,* she thumbed out. *Come by when you can. I know you're busy today.* She typed in the address and hit send.

Owen's next message said, *I miss you, Gina,* and filled her whole heart with hope. A smile touched her lips, and Gina left the arena with a bounce in her step that hadn't been there for months.

———

As the hours passed, Gina wondered if Owen would show up. She wasn't great in the kitchen, so she couldn't distract herself with baking. She didn't dare eat, in the hopes that he'd take her to dinner and profess his undying love for her.

She shook her head at her wishful thinking and moved onto the balcony that faced the beach. She didn't live beachside—not yet. Her three-bedroom cottage had it's own private beach, but she wanted new floors throughout and the whole thing painted before she moved in.

She'd been over to it every day in the past ten days since the sale had been accepted, and she was expanding the closet herself.

Leaning against the railing, she let the bay breeze trail across her face, a solid reminder that she loved this island and everything about it.

Including Owen.

A knock on the door had her spinning physically and mentally. "Just a minute," she called, hoping with everything inside her that it would be the tall, dreamy general manager on the other side.

Gina smoothed her hair and crossed through the kitchen and living room to open the door.

Owen stood there, his hands in his pockets and his head bent. He lifted his eyes to hers and drank her in without saying a single thing.

"I'm sorry," she blurted. "You probably hated that speech, but I couldn't think of anything big enough to let you know how honestly sorry I am."

Owen blinked, the only reaction at all. Gina felt like someone had shaken an entire six-pack of soda and opened them all at the same time inside her stomach.

"Will you please say something?"

Owen took one tiny step forward and then fell back again. "Are you moving here?"

Gina braced against the question and then relaxed. "This is my temporary apartment. I couldn't live at Sweet Breeze forever, even though their long-term apartment suites are *gorgeous*. Especially the closets." She grinned, hoping that he'd soften just a little. Take those hands out of his pockets and hold her close.

"But I bought a beach house, sort of down by you, actually. It's been abandoned for a while, so it needs some work. I should be able to move in by the end of June."

"Move in permanently." This time it wasn't a question, so maybe they were making progress.

"Yes, Owen. Permanently. I hired a new general manager for my Dallas office. They're going to handle the residential business, like we'd talked about. I have a couple of floors in that newly renovated building in east bay for my corporate closet division. I'm heading that up, right here in Getaway Bay."

Owen's eyes lit up. "Maybe you'll need a general manager for that. I happen to know a very good one."

Gina laughed, hoping that was the right response. "Please. Fisher would have kittens if I took you from Sweet Breeze. Plus, you'd be bored out of your mind. Right now, I only have one client."

"Hmm." He took that step again, this time committing to it. "You're resourceful. You'll have more in no time."

"I don't want you to be my general manager." Gina swallowed, her throat still a bit sticky and dry.

"No?"

"No." She shook her head and reached for the lapels on his jacket to draw him closer to her. "I want you to be my boyfriend. My partner in life. My best friend. My confidante. My lover."

That got him to finally soften, and he brought those hands and arms around her. Gina hadn't realized how much she'd missed him until he cradled her against his chest like she was something precious. He leaned his forehead against hers, the scent of him almost overpowering Gina's senses.

"Are you ready for all of that?" he asked, his breath whispering down the side of her face.

"I honestly don't know. But I can't keep pretending I'm not in love with you."

He pulled back and looked into her eyes, searching them for the truth, but Gina had already spoken it.

"It might take time," she said. "It's probably unfair of me to come back and ask for your forgiveness when I'm not sure I'm ready to take things farther than we already had."

But even as she spoke, Gina knew she was ready to move past where they'd been, truly invite him all the way inside her life.

"I don't mind waiting," Owen said. "But you have to talk to me. I didn't think I was a very needy guy, but I don't like the guessing games. The wondering. Maybe I'm just too old for that kind of stuff."

"I'm ready to talk," Gina said, her promises to Doctor White—her promises to *herself*—about to be kept. "But you might regret it. You might wish I'd shut up."

Owen grinned and shook his head. "I don't think so, sweetheart." He dipped his head toward hers as if he'd kiss her, stalling at the last moment. "Do we need to talk first, or can I kiss you?"

"Kiss me, please." Gina's eyes drifted closed, and the anticipation of kissing the man she loved was so delicious, she held onto the moment for as long as she could. Then she tipped up and matched her mouth to his.

# TWENTY-TWO

OWEN WATCHED Zach draw the packing tape over the top of the last box and stand back. "That's it." He looked around his bedroom where they'd been working for a few hours. Owen did too, a hint of pride mixing with his nerves.

"You can come stay anytime," Owen said. "Let's get these out to the truck."

Zach had arranged with Fisher to borrow one of the maintenance trucks from the hotel so he could move his stuff. He'd been assigned to live in a dorm with a couple of other guys from his high school, and one of their fathers had a boat. So if Zach could get his boxes to the boat, the three of them had gone in together to have a truck waiting on Oahu to get their belongings into their dorms.

Owen picked up a box and carried it around the corner. "Coop, we're loading up."

Cooper slid off the barstool and walked into Zach's room too, while Owen continued toward the front door. He rarely used this door, as he always pulled into the garage. He managed to get it open while juggling the box and he left it gaping behind him for his sons.

Together, they got all of Zach's boxes into the back of the pickup in about ten minutes. Owen looked at the few boxes and garbage bags full of towels and clothes. It seemed impossible that Zach could reduce his life to so little, but he didn't need any furniture for the dorm.

"If you find you need a car over there," Owen said. "Let me know. None of this secretive stuff like Maizee or being the valedictorian." He grinned at Zach. "Okay?"

Zach smiled back at him. "All right, Dad."

Owen let Zach get behind the wheel, and he waited for Cooper to slide into the middle of the bench seat before joining his sons in the cab of the truck. The drive down to the docks only took fifteen minutes, and Owen found himself wanting to hold onto Zach for just a little longer.

But he knew it was time to let him go, so Owen sat silently while Zach got out of the truck to talk to his friend. The other boy indicated the boat—which was a giant yacht —and Zach gestured for Cooper and Owen to come help him.

Owen took one garbage bag full of Zach's shirts and headed for the yacht. The other boy—Peter—showed Zach where to put his stuff, and where he'd be sleeping on the week-long journey toward Oahu.

Owen found Peter's father on the top deck and he introduced himself. "Thank you for doing this, Shawn," he said. "It's a huge help."

"No problem." The burly man had a quick smile and a

good air about him. "And they'll get a little vacation on the way. Seas are supposed to be calm."

Owen wasn't too terribly worried about the trip from island to island, but it was nice to know Shawn had at least checked the weather. And with a boat like this, he was obviously an experienced seaman.

"Let me give you my number," Owen said, pulling out his phone. "In case there are any issues on the yacht, or when you get to Oahu, with the truck." He dictated his number while Shawn typed it in and a moment later, Owen got a message from him. He saved the contact and turned toward the water.

It was a gloriously sunny day, and Owen felt the joy of the warm, golden light way down in his soul.

"Dad," Zach called, and Owen turned to leave.

"Thank you again."

"No problem, Owen." Shawn gave him another smile. "Did you get back together with Gina?"

Owen turned back to him, surprise flowing freely through him.

"I was at graduation. Good speech your boy gave."

"Oh, yes." Owen smiled too. "Thank you." He started down to the main deck. "And yes, I got back together with Gina."

He found Zach near the plank leading back to land, and they walked off the boat together. "All right," Owen said, sighing. "I guess this is good-bye for a while."

"Just a couple of months," Zach said. "I'll come home for a week before fall semester starts."

Owen wrapped his oldest son in a hug, memories flying

through his mind like bullets. There were so many mile-stones—his first word, first step, first lost tooth, first day of school. So many happy memories of them at the beach, snorkeling, going to luaus, taking hikes up to the lava cliffs.

This was just another one. Another first. Another step in a life that would hopefully be wonderful and good.

"Love you, Zach," Owen said, the hitch in his voice obvious. He didn't even try to hide it.

Zach hugged Cooper too, a little tighter and a little longer than he did Owen, and then he finally stepped back. "I'll call you," he said. "Whenever I have service, okay?"

Owen nodded and put his arm around Cooper's shoulders. They trembled a little, testifying that his youngest son was really struggling. Owen didn't know how to help him other than to do exactly what Zach had told all the seniors at his high school to do: Be there.

Zach disappeared onto the yacht with his friends, and Owen took a few deep breaths. "Well, should we get some lunch?"

———

Two weeks later, Owen found himself moving more boxes, this time for Gina as she moved out of her temporary apartment and into her beach cottage. The house sat only two miles from Owen's home, a fact he'd noted silently and kept to himself.

She'd had the inside completely redone, from the flooring, to the paint, to the furnishings. It was light and airy and perfectly Gina. The house had three bedrooms, and she set up one as hers and one as an office.

"What about this last one?" Owen asked.

"Oh, maybe I'll have guests one day," she said lightly, breezing out the door to get another item and bring it into the house.

Sasha and Lexie both moved around the kitchen, unpacking boxes while their husbands carried in the couch, a rocking chair, a desk, and more boxes. Owen felt somewhat adrift, but he managed to keep himself busy though he mostly stood by Gina while she gave directions to the other men.

Once all the big stuff was in, Gina called and ordered pizza for everyone, and an unpacking party began. Owen knew she wouldn't be able to sleep tonight if there was a single item out of place, though he had seen her apartment a few days ago and it had looked like a bomb had gone off. So maybe she'd eased up a bit on her controlling tendencies.

They'd spent a lot of time talking over the past month since Zach's graduation. A lot of time on the beach with each other. He'd finally taken her to get that snorkeling gear and they'd spent time exploring life under the ocean. Life with each other, too.

They'd have a very serious conversation about children when Stacey had shown up to the Beach Club with an announcement that she and Fisher were expecting their first child next winter.

*I don't want kids, Owen.*

Her voice rang through his mind as loudly now as it had

then. He handed her a stack of plates, and she turned to survey the cupboards before deciding on one.

Owen didn't particularly want more children—he'd just sent his adult son off to college—but he'd have done whatever Gina had wanted. And she didn't want children, and Owen was fine with that.

She still saw her therapist every week, but the difference was, she told him about it. Worked through things with him instead of holding him on the fringes of her life. And if it were possible, he'd fallen even more in love with her.

"Pizza's here," Jasper announced, and Owen breathed a sigh of relief. He worked hard at Sweet Breeze but it was nothing like packing and moving, which he'd done twice now in a short period of time.

He thought about the diamond Jasper had helped him pick out a couple of days ago. He hadn't brought it to Gina's beach cottage, knowing full-well that she was not ready to get engaged. But Owen wanted to be ready at the first sign that she *was* ready, and he thought he'd have a pretty good idea of when that was.

It didn't happen in July, or August, and as September came to a close and Gina worked feverishly to finish the last closet at the hotel, Owen wondered if maybe he should just give up on the idea of getting married before he turned fifty.

His forty-seventh birthday was just around the corner, and well, he wouldn't exactly be surprised if it took three years to get Gina down the aisle.

"Maybe I should just ask her," he muttered to himself as he left his office.

"Ask who what?" Fisher stood there with Stacey, his arm

around her carefully like she couldn't even walk now that she was carrying a baby.

"Nothing," Owen said. "What can I do for you?"

"We heard Zach's coming home for Christmas, and we want to host on the twenty-eighth floor," Stacey said. "You, the boys, Gina."

"Just the six of us?" Owen asked. "What about Lexie and Sasha and all the others?"

"Lexie and Sasha are going on a cruise with Gabi," Stacey said. "Jasper and Jason are going too, obviously. Esther is spending the holidays with Marshall's parents. So it's just us, and we'd like to have you and the boys with us." She smiled at him in that loving, sisterly way that Owen needed in his life.

"I'll talk to Gina." He started to move past Stacey and Fisher.

"About Christmas," Stacey said. "And that ring you keep in your top drawer."

Owen spun back to them, his eyes wide. "You told her?" He couldn't look away from Fisher.

He chuckled. "Look, she has a way of learning things," Fisher said. "It's not my fault."

Owen's anger faded as quickly as it had reared. "I want to ask her, but I'm not sure she's ready."

"Why don't you find out?" Fisher opened Owen's office and went inside. He returned a few seconds later with the black jewelry box. "You won't know until you ask."

"Let her tell you if she's ready or not," Stacey said. "Maybe she's just waiting for you to ask."

Owen took the box with numb fingers. "I was just on my

way up to see her. She should have the last closet done today."

"Go on, then." Fisher's kind smile seemed a bit at odds with his wolfish grin.

Owen took the ring out of the box and slipped it into his breast pocket. He handed the box to Stacey and said, "This could be a huge mistake."

"Or a huge win," she said.

The ring felt like a brand over Owen's heart. "All right. Here I go."

"Text us!" Fisher called after him, but Owen had to focus all his energy on walking and couldn't respond.

# TWENTY-THREE

GINA LINED up the last hanger, knowing it would get moved the moment the client entered the closet. She didn't care. This was the last closet at Sweet Breeze, the end of a huge, seven-month project that she'd busted her back to finish on time.

Satisfaction sang through her, despite the fact that tomorrow, she didn't have another job lined up. She needed some time off after putting in eighteen-hour days for the last three weeks.

Stepping back, she said, "It's done." A smile accompanied the statement, and she wished Owen were beside her. He was due to arrive any moment, and Gina stood in the closet hoping he'd get there soon.

"Gina," he said from behind her, and she left the closet and hurried through the bedroom.

"Come see," she said. "It's done."

Owen grinned at her, because it wasn't like he hadn't

seen this exact closet several times already. But he humored her, took her hand in his, and let her lead him into the master closet she'd finished in half the time she thought she could.

"Stunning," Owen said. "As always." He drew her into his side and admired the closet, just the way Gina wanted him to. He didn't feel as relaxed as he usually did, and she glanced at him.

"How's Zach?"

"Doing great. Got there. Got unpacked. Found a job."

And now he was speaking in very short sentences. Not good.

"Gina, I wanted to talk to you about something."

Of course he did, and Gina actually liked that he did. "All right."

"You can say whatever you feel, as always."

"I will." Her anxiety started to rise, just like it always did when Owen brought her a serious conversation topic. They'd had so many important discussions, and Gina only knew of one more that needed to happen.

Owen shifted so that he stood in front of her. He reached into his breast pocket and pulled out a diamond ring.

Gina gasped, sucking at the air. "Owen."

"I don't want to rush you," he said, keeping his head ducked and his eyes on the glittering gem. "But I'm in love with you, and I want you to be my wife." He finally lifted his eyes to hers, and Gina let his words roll through her.

*Wife.*

She'd never wanted to be a wife.

But she did want to be *Owen's* wife, and that was a big distinction.

"What do you think?" he asked. "Jasper helped me pick it out, and I've just been holding onto it while I watched to see if you might be ready. But then...." He shrugged, and he was absolutely adorable.

"I thought maybe we could at least start talking about it."

"We can talk about it."

He moved to put the ring away, and she said, "Wait, whoa, wait. Where are you putting that?"

Their eyes locked, and Gina wasn't sure what she was saying. So Owen's next question—"What are you saying?"—was really hard to answer.

"I—I mean...I love you, too." She reached up and stroked her hand down the side of his face. "You know that, right?"

"I do know that." Owen leaned forward and kissed her quickly. "Tell me what you're afraid of. What's worrying you about us getting married."

"Living arrangements," Gina said, almost blurting it out. "I just bought my place, and I know it's stupid, but I love being right on the beach. But I can't—I won't—take Cooper out of his childhood home."

Owen nodded. "It's a valid concern."

Gina was sure he'd thought about it too. After all, no one knew her better than Owen.

"What else?" he asked.

Gina wound her hands around the back of his neck. "You know what? There is nothing else."

Owen's lips curved up and he said, "I have a solution for your living arrangements problem."

Gina giggled. "I'm sure you do."

"I don't want to dislodge Cooper either. So I propose we get married as fast as possible." He bent his head toward hers and kissed her, capturing her lips completely and telling her how much he wanted her. Wanted her in his home, in his life…in his bed.

"And then you move in with us." His voice came out as barely a whisper. "Keep the beach house. We'll go down there all the time. Run the two miles down to the beach, make coffee, enjoy the sunrise, and run home to get ready for the day."

He kissed her again, and Gina really liked his solution so far. "And then?"

"And then, once Cooper moves on with his life, we'll move to your place together. Make it *our* home, right there on the beach." He swayed back and forth, and Gina would dance anywhere with him. Including the couple of miles up the road to his house until Cooper was finished with high school.

Gina closed her eyes and imagined dancing with him like this while she wore a white dress. It was everything she wanted, and not a stitch of fear existed inside her.

"All right, Owen," she said, pulling back and gazing up at him. "I'll marry you."

His eyes lit up. "Yeah? Don't sound so excited about it."

She laughed, tipping her head back and letting him hold her around the waist. She sobered and met his eye. "I love you, Owen. Of course I want to marry you."

"As soon as possible." He grinned. "I fell in love with

you right here in a closet like this one, and I can't wait to make a life with you."

Tears pricked Gina's eyes, and she kissed Owen like she'd never kissed him before. "Will you put that ring on my finger now, please?"

Owen chuckled as he slid the ring on her left hand and then kissed her like he really, truly loved her.

Gina soaked him in, never wanted to be without him, and pulled away with a grin. "Do you think Christmas is soon enough for a wedding?"

"Sweetheart, I'd marry you tomorrow."

"Well, I think the ladies in the Beach Club would kill me if we did that. Christmas is only three months away." A blip of panic pulsed through her. Three months.

"I guess I can wait three more months," Owen said, kissing her again, and with the weight of the ring on her finger, Gina had never been happier in her life.

———

Read on for a sneak peek of the first chapter of
**RAINFOREST RETREAT, the next book in the Getaway
Bay Resort Romance series.**

# SNEAK PEEK! RAINFOREST RETREAT CHAPTER ONE

THE WIND PICKED up as Maizee Phelps came up over the rise of the hill, the beautiful Umauma Waterfall spreading out before her. With her breathing coming quickly, Maizee felt a rush of accomplishment.

She liked nothing better than being outside, among the trees and foliage of Hawaii, the wide, blue sky above her.

Except today, the weather wasn't exactly friendly. With Tropical Storm Eric on the horizon, Maizee supposed she should've been at her new apartment, making sure she had enough groceries for the next few days, and hunkering down.

But she'd just arrived in Getaway Bay three days ago, and she didn't want to spend her weekend before starting at the bank indoors. No, if she could, she'd be out in a kayak, exploring this island she'd only visited as a tourist in the past.

Her calves tightened, but she kept walking until she

found the perfect sketching spot. To her left, she could see the falls, and to her right, the horizon showed the edge of the island and then the gorgeous Pacific Ocean. And way out where the sea kissed the sky, the darkness indicated Eric was indeed alive and well.

The storm wasn't set to hit the island for another day, at least, and Maizee wasn't worried. As a Hawaii native from the island of Lanai, she'd weathered plenty of storms. Too bad she wasn't as good at surviving the relationship disasters in her life.

She sighed as she swung the backpack off her shoulders and set it at her feet. "And you thought Winn was the one." She shook her head, wishing she was brave enough to stay at the same branch as him, face him everyday, and just carry on with her life.

Maybe find someone new, fall madly in love, and show him that he hadn't affected her all that much.

Unfortunately, he had become her whole world over the past five years—one of which where she wore his diamond ring—and she didn't have the stomach to see him each day at work and not go home with him at night.

At least he'd broken things off before she'd booked a wedding venue. She did, however, have a white gown that she now had no use for. She'd asked her mother if she could store it in her childhood closet, and that was where it currently hung.

Maizee figured she'd try to sell it one day, perhaps when the memories containing Winn didn't make her chest pinch and her whole countenance sad.

She unzipped her pack and pulled out her sketchpad

before tipping her chin toward the sky. She rolled her shoulders and took a long drink of water from her bottle, moving through her muscles as they started to cool.

Once she had relaxed, she reached back into her pack and found the box of black crayons she took everywhere with her.

She didn't care that Winn had labeled her art "colorless" and "kind of weird." Maizee loved the way crayon could be sharp and thin, or thick, jagged lines, with no defined edges. She felt like the black crayon, sometimes with every piece of jewelry and strand of hair in the exact right place, and sometimes with her hair in a messy bun and more pizza sauce on her T-shirt and fingers than on the actual pie.

"Sit down, Roger," she told her little dog, and the long-haired Jack Russell terrier complied, his tongue hanging out of his mouth. She poured him a bit of water into a collapsible bowl, and the dog lapped at it without standing up.

Maizee drained the rest of the water bottle, hoping she'd make it back to the trailhead before she had to use the restroom, and set the sketchpad on her knees. She always started with the sharpest crayons, and she roughed in the falls, the trees, and the horizon beyond them before switching to a duller one to add in the softer parts of the picture.

She realized how whippy the wind had become when she shivered, the sweat on her neck and forehead chilly now. Glancing up, she found the sky darkening, clouds rolling in from the black spot on the horizon.

Startled, Maizee dropped the crayon she'd been using to add in the finer details. Her heart thumped a bit painfully in her chest. This storm had blown in quickly, and she hadn't even seen it coming.

It certainly wasn't Eric, but she still didn't want to be on this unfamiliar trail in the dark or the rain. She took a few precious seconds to make sure she had everything she'd brought, including every last crayon shaving. Then she shouldered her pack and clipped Roger to the carabiner on her strap, saying, "Let's go, boy."

She cast one last look at the falls she'd been drawing before starting down the path she'd come up. It was only a mile and a half, but she hadn't been in a hurry on the way up. She was now, and the stormclouds continued to steal the light from the day with every step she took.

She estimated she was about halfway down when the first drops of rain splashed against her face. Pausing, she swung her backpack off and dug around inside it for the emergency poncho she never left home without. It was clear, but it would keep her dry, and Maizee knew better than most that it was astronomically better to be dry than it was to be wet. Especially with the wind as strong as it was.

"Come on," she said to the little dog, using him to keep herself centered. She couldn't panic, as that had never helped, and she needed a cool head if she was going to make it back to her car in one piece.

"It's just a little rain, Roger. We'll be okay." But she wasn't comforted by the little rivulets of mud racing down the side of the path with her. She kept to the rockier parts of the trail, thinking the stones would give her the traction she needed as the rain really started to drive down now.

Maizee could barely see in front of her, but she didn't

want to slow down. Gravity seemed to pull on her, helping her get down the trail to the parking lot. She felt near panic, but she just kept moving.

*One more step*, she thought, her breath sticking somewhere inside her chest. Over and over, she thought it. Kept breathing. She may have offered up a prayer.

And then her one more step went awry, and her ankle twisted painfully. She yelped, threw her arms out in front of her as if there would be something for her to grab onto, and realized she was going down.

She landed on the ground on her hands and knees and quickly rolled onto her backside. The rain made such a ruckus against the plastic poncho, and Roger yowled too.

"Roger," she said, barely able to see the dog. He limped over to her, and a sense of helplessness that felt bottomless filled her. She cradled the little dog while she tried to catch her breath.

Once she did, she tried to look at her ankle, but everything was coated in mud. Pain thrummed through her foot and leg with every beat of her heart, and she had no idea what to do.

"Get up," she told herself through gritted teeth. "You can't lie here in the mud and wait for someone to find you."

There was no one to find her. She hadn't passed a single person going up or down to the falls, and while Maizee had felt utterly alone before, this was a whole new level of isolation. Tears sprang to her eyes, but she refused to let them out. Crying never helped anything. It didn't get her job back. Didn't help get her boyfriend back. Didn't make her boss do much of anything but transfer her to a new branch on a different island in the hopes that "a fresh start" would be what she needed.

But right now, she needed the rain to stop and the sun to come back out. She needed a warm bath and then a warmer blanket.

Roger barked, a high-pitched yelp that Maizee imagined meant, "Help!" in canine. He squirmed away from her and trotted away until the leash tightened. He barked again, facing down the path instead of up toward the falls the way Maizee was.

"I can get up," she told him, but he continued to yap like his life depended on it. Maizee braced both hands against the slick mud and pushed herself over onto her knees. Now, she just needed to get her feet under her, and she'd get back to her car and assess the damage from there.

Balanced on her hands and knees, she put her weight on her good foot, and pushed. As pressure came down on her injured ankle, it buckled again. She cried out, which sent Roger into a tizzy, and sank back to the earth.

She let a few tears out now, mostly because of the white-hot pain in her foot, but also because she couldn't see an acceptable way out of this dilemma. No one even knew where she was. No one in her neighborhood even knew her name. She'd spent the three days she'd been on this island getting her house set up and filling it with food and basic home goods.

Her new job started on Monday, and she'd been looking forward to a relaxing weekend before her real life had to start again.

No one would see the tears among the rain anyway. There wasn't anyone to see anything.

And yet, Roger barked like he was sending a message to someone, somewhere. Maizee tried to shush him, but he would not be silenced. So she ignored him while she took off her pack and started rummaging around inside. Maybe she could make something that would support her ankle enough to get her off this trail.

She took a couple of painkillers, and the simple nature of the action calmed her a little. Taking a deep breath, she pulled out her first aid kit, wishing she'd had the foresight to put a brace inside. But all she had were Bandaids, moleskin, gauze and medical tape, and hand sanitizer. She had the sketchpad and the crayons, as well as a length of rope, a pair of nail clippers, and a bag of the peppermint mints she liked to suck on while she hiked.

And a tall Gatorade bottle.

She pulled it out and grabbed the medical tape. She couldn't fit the bottle down into her shoe, but she turned it upside down so the narrower end was at her heel and she taped the bottle to her ankle and leg, the pressure painful until she moved up higher on her calf.

"All right," she said, once again praying her makeshift brace would help. She zipped everything back inside her pack and tried to stand again. She got to her feet this time, but stood on the path, the toe on her injured foot barely touching the ground as she balanced on her other foot.

She didn't see how she could take a step on her injured leg, Gatorade bottle or not. She took a deep breath and prepared herself to fall again when she heard a distinct voice calling through the rain.

"Hello? Is anyone there?"

"I'm here," she yelled, her voice more shrill than she liked. But at this point, she couldn't care. "Up here. I'm up here!"

A figure came through the rain, becoming more and more defined with every step up the trail he took.

He was a tall man, wearing a hooded jacket and a pair of jeans. At least he wore a decent pair of shoes as he came closer and closer.

"I did hear a dog," he said as Roger jumped up on him, marring his pants with mud. Maizee should've corrected her animal, but she honestly couldn't look away from the man who'd miraculously showed up to save her.

She knew him. Lawrence Gladstone—the owner of the bank where she'd worked for the past nineteen years.

No, they had never met in person—she would've remembered that. But everyone who worked at Gladstone Financial knew who Lawrence was.

"Are you okay?" His dark, dreamy eyes ran from her foot to her face and back again. "You have a bottle taped to your leg." He had to shout to be heard over the rain, but that only ensured that Maizee could hear the bass quality of his voice.

"I fell down," she said, wondering why he could look like male perfection in a rainstorm while she surely looked like a drowned rat. "Twisted my ankle."

"Can you walk?"

"I don't think so. I just barely managed to get up." She

tugged on Roger's leash to get him to settle down, but the dog seemed as anxious to get off this trail as Maizee was.

"Well, let's see what we can do." He stepped to her side, and she admired the neat beard and mustache he wore. "I'm going to put my arm around you." He did, and she lifted hers over his shoulders with a groan.

"Okay, let's try." He stepped and she tried, but her ankle was not accepting any weight and she almost pulled them both to the ground.

Lawrence grunted and steadied her before taking a step back. "All right, so that's out." He glanced around. "We better find somewhere to ride out this storm. Then I can make a call."

Of course he could. She was surprised he hadn't already, that the Coast Guard, all the officers at the naval base on the island, and every local cop, paramedic, and firefighter weren't already on their way here.

Instead of saying anything, she just nodded as if she knew a good spot where they could ride out the storm. But she didn't.

————

**Read RAINFOREST RETREAT today!** You'll get to see a billionaire who has a love affair with his job, his new bank manager, and how they bravely navigate the island of Getaway Bay!

# BOOKS IN THE GETAWAY BAY RESORT ROMANCE SERIES

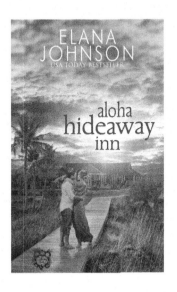

**Aloha Hideaway Inn (Book 1):** Can Stacey and the Aloha Hideaway Inn survive strange summer weather, the arrival of the new resort, *and* the start of a special relationship?

**Getaway Bay (Book 2):** Can Esther deal with dozens of business tasks, unhappy tourists, *and* the twists and turns in her new relationship?

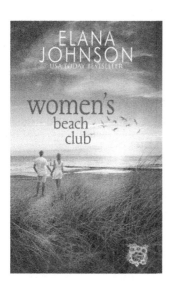

**Women's Beach Club (Book 3):** With the help of her friends in the Beach Club, can Tawny solve the mystery, stay safe, and keep her man?

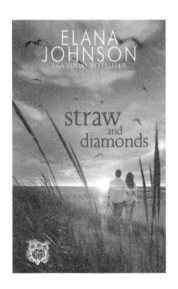

**Straw and Diamonds (Book 4):** Can Sasha maintain her sanity amidst their busy schedules, her issues with men like Jasper, and her desires to take her business to the next level?

**The Billionaire Club (Book 5):** Can Lexie keep her business affairs in the shadows while she brings her relationship out of them? Or will she have to confess everything to her new friends...and Jason?

**Sweet Breeze Resort (Book 6):** Can Gina manage her business across the sea and finish the remodel at Sweet Breeze, all while developing a meaningful relationship with Owen and his sons?

**Rainforest Retreat (Book 7):** As their paths continue to cross and Lawrence and Maizee spend more and more time together, will he find in her a retreat from all the family pressure? Can Maizee manage her relationship with her boss, or will she once again put her heart—and her job—on the line?

**Getaway Bay Singles (Book 8):** Can Katie bring him into her life, her daughter's life, and manage her business while he manages the app? Or will everything fall apart for a second time?

Turn the page to view series starters from three of my other series!

# BOOKS IN THE GETAWAY BAY ROMANCE SERIES

Escape to Getaway Bay and meet your new best friends as these women navigate their careers, their love lives, and their own dreams and desires. Each heartwarming love story shows the power of women in their own lives and the lives of their friends.

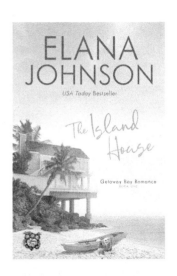

**The Island House (Book 1):** Charlotte Madsen's whole world came crashing down six months ago with the words, "I met someone else."

**Can Charlotte navigate the healing process to find love again?**

# BOOKS IN THE STRANDED IN GETAWAY BAY ROMANCE SERIES

Meet the McLaughlin Sisters in Getaway Bay as they encounter disaster after disaster...including the men they get stranded with. From ex-boyfriends to cowboys to football stars, these sisters can bring any man to his knees when the cards are stacked against them.

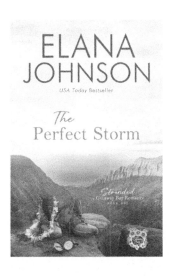

**The Perfect Storm (Book 1):** A freak storm has her sliding down the mountain...right into the arms of her ex. As Eden and Holden spend time out in the wilds of Hawaii trying to survive, their old flame is rekindled. But with secrets and old feelings in the way, will Holden be able to take all the broken pieces of his life and put them back together in a way that makes sense? Or will he lose his heart and the reputation of his company because of a single landslide?

# BOOKS IN THE CARTER'S COVE ROMANCE SERIES

Visit the South Carolina coast and The Heartwood Inn in these clean and wholesome beach romances. Each romance features a Heartwood sister navigating the potholes of romance with someone they DEFINITELY don't get along with...

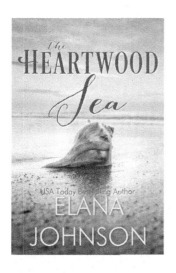

**The Heartwood Sea (Book 1):** She owns The Heartwood Inn. He needs the land the inn sits on to impress his boss. Neither one of them will give an inch. But will they give each other their hearts?

# ABOUT ELANA

Elana Johnson is the USA Today bestselling and Kindle All-Star author of dozens of clean and wholesome contemporary romance novels. She lives in Utah, where she mothers two fur babies, works with her husband full-time, and eats a lot of veggies while writing. Find her on her website at feelgoodfictionbooks.com

Made in United States
North Haven, CT
05 February 2024

48348876R00157